A fantasy. He is a fantasy.

Because it had always been him, hadn't it?

Constantine was the one who had appealed to her in this darkly sexual way that had always felt shameful to her.

Morgan had always been so ashamed of this part of herself. The part of her that didn't simply want sweet and wonderful words, but wanted a man who wanted her. A man who would grab hold of her with big, strong hands. A man who would kiss her, taste her...

She had pushed all that down and told herself that she didn't need that sort of thing.

Because it kept her safe.

Because it felt like something that was too close to her mother and all of her vices.

There was that word again.

Vices.

Perhaps beauty was his. And *he* was hers.

And she would make herself a slave to it. For tonight. Just tonight.

Millie Adams has always loved books. She considers herself a mix of Anne Shirley (loquacious but charming and willing to break a slate over a boy's head if need be) and Charlotte Doyle (a lady at heart but with the spirit to become a mutineer should the occasion arise). Millie lives in a small house on the edge of the woods, which she finds allows her to escape in the way she loves best— in the pages of a book. She loves intense alpha heroes and the women who dare to go toe-to-toe with them (or break a slate over their heads).

Books by Millie Adams

Harlequin Presents

The Kings of California

The Scandal Behind the Italian's Wedding
Stealing the Promised Princess
Crowning His Innocent Assistant
The Only King to Claim Her

Visit the Author Profile page
at Harlequin.com for more titles.

Millie Adams

—

HIS SECRETLY PREGNANT CINDERELLA

Recycling programs
for this product may
not exist in your area.

ISBN-13: 978-1-335-56933-2

His Secretly Pregnant Cinderella

Copyright © 2022 by Millie Adams

This edition published by arrangement with Harlequin Books S.A.

For questions and comments about the quality of this book, please contact us at CustomerService@Harlequin.com.

Harlequin Enterprises ULC
22 Adelaide St. West, 41st Floor
Toronto, Ontario M5H 4E3, Canada
www.Harlequin.com

Printed in U.S.A.

HIS SECRETLY PREGNANT CINDERELLA

To the Harlequin Presents line. For all the joy, fantasy and escape it's provided me, both as a reader and a writer.

CHAPTER ONE

Morgan Stanfield had never taken seriously the idea that a person could die of embarrassment. But from where she was crouched currently, dressed in nothing but a black lace bodysuit, watching her boyfriend of approximately six months laying another woman down onto the bed, she was sure that she was close.

And that, perhaps, should have been the first clue that it was actually a good thing that Alex was cheating on her. Really, she should've known.

She should have known that whatever patience he seemed to have for her desire to wait, he would not defer his own pleasure endlessly. She should have known he didn't actually love her quite so much.

And Morgan had always wondered why he'd been with her. She had always wondered why Alex was interested in her. She had met him when she was waitressing at a bar near her university, and she had been shocked when he'd approached her. He was tall and beautiful with arresting dark eyes and an easy smile. His Greek accent had sent shivers down her spine.

Morgan had worked for everything that she'd ever received in her life, and she was not working at the bar by the university because she went to the university. It was because she wanted to. Because she was saving up all of her precious money to get herself a better future. And when she'd started dating Alex, that future had suddenly been dropped in her lap. He'd given her the funds to go to school immediately, even though she had protested. He had brought her to family functions, bought her clothes and paid for her to be transported to luxurious affairs, and never once had he pressured her for sex.

Well, now she could see why.

He was getting it elsewhere.

And she was… Devastated.

She was also trapped. Trapped in her boyfriend's bedroom at his parents' house, their estate, actually, about to see a whole lot more sex than she'd ever had in her life. And she really thought she might die. She really did. And that was when she turned and saw the door that led out onto the balcony. The alcove she was in was quite separate from the bedroom. These rooms were more like suites, with separate compartments. And she had a feeling that if she crawled over to the door, and worked her way out onto the balcony, she would be able to go unnoticed.

Granted, once she was out there she might be stuck, but she would prefer that to being stuck indoors with a full pornographic scene happening within earshot. She took a breath. She turned and began to crawl across the floor. Literally crawl on her belly. Well, her friends had been right. Men like him were too good to be true, and it could only end in humiliation.

Of course, she hadn't confessed to her friends that she hadn't given him her virginity yet.

They thought she was silly being a virgin as it was, much less when she had a gorgeous, rich boyfriend. It was just that she'd seen the way that men had taken advantage of her mother over the years, and she had never wanted to… She had never wanted to lose herself like that. Had never wanted to lose her mind quite to that degree.

That worked out well, didn't it?

She could finally touch the door. She reached up and prayed that the handle would pull. It did. Easily, and she was able to get it open silently. Staying low, she wiggled through the crack she created in the doorway, then once she was outside, keeping the handle pressed down, reached up and close it as silently as she had opened it to begin with.

She sat crouched on the balcony.

This was stupid. It was absolutely stupid. She had finally thought to…to give herself to him and he was giving himself to someone else. She wondered if his parents had any idea he had a woman here…

She knew who probably did. A dark rage expanded in her chest. Oh, yes, she was sure that there was one person who was well aware that Alex was locked away in his suite with some blond beauty.

His older brother.

The man who hated her most of all.

The man whose name she would not even think. Because he didn't deserve it.

In her moment of humiliation, acknowledging his existence would be too great a burden to bear.

She looked down below. She was four stories up, and she did not relish the idea of trying to climb down.

Then, she really would be dead ostensibly of humiliation, and that seemed a fate too ignominious to contend with.

She looked across and saw that she was very close to the next balcony. She was trying to remember what the room might be, based on her time spent in the manor. A library, maybe. Or was that on the other side? Honestly, it didn't much matter. She just needed to look in and see if it was occupied.

She stood up slowly, certain that Alex and his lover would be too occupied to notice if there was movement outside, and looked across the space between the stone railings. Honestly, in any other circumstance, she would have called herself crazy, curled up in a ball and lain there on the floor of the balcony until someone came to rescue her. But, no one was going to rescue her. Not from this, not from the site of her own folly. She would have to rescue herself. There was no rescuing her pride. It was already on the ground. So, she would think nothing about crossing the two spaces. She would have not a care in the world about falling.

"Don't do that," she said to herself, "if you fall to the ground you won't die, it's grass. You'll only be maimed. And that's really only compounding the problem, isn't it?"

She gritted her teeth, and before she could talk herself out of it, lifted herself up and slung one leg across the railing on her balcony, and over the railing on the next, not quite able to plant her foot on the floor of the next balcony, but feeling somewhat secure that she at least had herself partially there. Then she lifted herself with her arms, and planted the next leg over, rocking forward and pitching herself safely to the ground. Thank God.

She really didn't want to have to do that again. She looked next door and saw that the room was dim. There was no movement, though, she could not tell quite which room it was. There were bookcases, so perhaps she was right, and it was the library. Her only hope was that the door was also unlocked to this balcony. And it was. She slipped in quickly and quietly, cursing that she had left all of her clothes behind. She moaned. He was going to wonder about the clothes. Later, it was going to be clear someone else had been there. Or maybe he wouldn't notice. Maybe he would attribute it to some other fling. Or maybe the maid would clean it up before he ever saw them.

It didn't much matter, because she was never going to see him again. Not him or anyone from this family. For a moment, she felt utterly, desolately sad. Because she had been convinced that… That she'd found a dream.

But dreams did not come true for girls like her. Not dreams like this. There was no Prince Charming. There was no magical happy ending; there was just not going to be any getting out of this with her dignity. But all she needed to do was get down the stairs. And out the front door. And if she had to run… Well, there could only ever be a rumor of a crazed redhead running through the halls. She would never look back, she would never call back, and she would go back to being alone… It was just all over. All of it.

She took a step deeper into the room and heard a sound. A glass clicking against a hard surface.

"Well. When I ordered a nightcap, I can honestly say I did not expect this."

"Constantine."

Because of course it was him. Of course, he would be the one to see. Of course, he would be the one in this room.

She was surprised he didn't bring with him hell's very fire and all the demons. Or maybe he had, because she was suddenly hot.

He's always made you hot…

She ignored that. As she'd ignored the heat for six months. Because Constantine wasn't her knight in shining armor. Her Prince Charming.

Constantine was something shameful, dark and awful she pretended she didn't harbor inside of herself.

Alex isn't your Prince Charming either…

"So it is you. I thought that I recognized you." His dark gaze swept over her, the contempt there so…

Obvious.

Scathing.

Hot.

"I see you've abandoned your fresh-faced in-genue look for the evening." The expression on his face was almost bland. If you didn't know him.

And, sadly, she did.

She had made an effort to not know him, but it was unavoidable.

Over the past six months she had been taken into the family with enthusiasm. She loved Alex's parents.

She did not love Constantine. And he did not love her.

But she was fascinated by him. She had learned to read a lot of things in one quirk of his arrogant eyebrow, had become well acquainted with the disapproval inherent in the slightest adjustment of his jacket cuff. He did not look at her so much as through her, so at this moment, as he looked at her with that burning intensity, she felt it. Down to the very center of her soul.

"Your brother is otherwise occupied," she said.

And if a person could die of humiliation then she was well on her way.

Because to have to admit to Constantine Kamaras of all people, that she was… That she had been replaced… Not even replaced, as she had never even been in Alex's bed.

Your choice, Morgan.

Yes, it was her choice. Born out of extreme paranoia, to be sure. A fear that if she were to fall pregnant she wouldn't be taken care of, that she would end up like her mother.

But she had gotten so… So confident in Alex. And what they had. And she had been ready to…

It was more than humiliation that had her reeling now. It was the stunning clarity that in her confidence in another person she had still been wrong. But she had been cautious all this time and so certain of him…

And she had been wrong.

"He is otherwise occupied?"

He shifted in his chair, affecting a more languid pose than she ever typically associated with Constantine. He was rigid. Hard like a mountain. And yet at the moment he looked… Approachable. Which made him all the more terrifying.

His shirt collar was open, revealing a wedge of chest, a bit of dark hair. His sleeves were pushed up to his elbows, and she couldn't help but take stock of his muscular forearms.

He had the sculpted face of a fallen angel.

His eyes black as midnight, and his hair like a raven's wing.

He was every gothic fantasy a lonely girl growing up with books and little else for comfort could have ever wanted.

Pity he hated her.

Pity he was the older brother of the love of her life.

Pity the love of her life was a faithless scoundrel.

And really, the biggest pity of all was the fact that she was standing there in her underwear.

"What an effect," he said, his tone dark. "You in that, and with the man you intended to seduce occupied. I feel I must ask. Is it another woman who occupies his attentions?"

"Yes." She did her best to copy his uncaring pose. "And I think you know that."

She let one shoulder drop, and with it went the strap on the shockingly scandalous teddy she was wearing. Absurdly one piece and all lace so you could see her body peeking from beneath rose petals in a rather strategic fashion.

It had seemed so daring and sensual earlier.

Now it just seemed dangerous.

"I know nothing of the comings and goings of my brother, mainly because if I had to keep tabs on every creature he took into his bed I would do nothing else. You must understand,

Morgan, my objection to you has always been that you were simply another in a long line of questionable choices my brother seems to enjoy making."

She refused to let the words stab her.

"He loves you, you know," Morgan said. "He thinks you are the most brilliant, wonderful man in the entire world."

"What is it they say?" Constantine said, looking down at his hands for a moment, and then back up at her. "Yes. Imitation is the sincerest form of flattery. And my younger brother is hardly even a pantomime of me. And I think *you* know that."

There was something about that dark, disdainful note in his voice that sent a shiver directly down her spine. And to her horror, her nipples beaded tight behind the lace bra that did not do an effective job of covering her breasts.

"I think I would like to hear the story of how you came to be standing here without your clothes."

"I told you. I... Well. I..." And this was where it was going to be tricky to keep her pride.

Your pride is shot to hell, Morgan, you might as well tell him. He thinks the worst of you. Go ahead and give him a story.

"I decided to sneak in his room tonight. To surprise him. Unfortunately I learned the hard way that there are some men you should not surprise. I went into the bathroom to change... And I was in the corner of his room in the dark when he arrived with... Whoever she is." Her stomach was like acid. "And my clothing was in a different room. I could not bear the thought of him seeing me so I slipped out the balcony. I could not climb straight down, so I decided to seek another room that I might enter... And as you can see it turned out to be occupied. So. Surprises all around."

"That is quite the tale," he said. And there was nothing but silence between them as he looked at her. Behind every petal, she felt. "It would be a shame to waste the outfit, don't you think?"

Her stomach plummeted, that place between her legs began to pulse in a strange and greedy fashion.

She had been ready to sleep with Alex, and she had not felt like this. But one look of intent from Constantine and her entire body was thrown into a tailspin.

You read too many fantastical novels when you were a girl. You are being a fool.

No. Maybe she wasn't being a fool. After all, she had been certain of Alex, and it was over. It was over. And that realization washed over her like a wave. Insistent and terrible.

He was sleeping with another woman. And she could never...

She could never subject herself to that. And it did not matter that he had paid for her schooling. It did not matter that she loved his family.

She wanted to be loved.

Morgan Stanfield had never been beloved in her entire life. She had been a burden to her mother, nothing to whoever her father was... And she had been certain she had finally found love with Alex. With his family.

But he did not love her. She didn't know what game he was playing with her, but it was clear that it had to be a game. It had to be.

And she was an idiot who did not have any kind of special insight into other people. Who was not more responsible than other women, than her mother. She had been ready to fling herself on that ghastly altar of love because she had finally thought that she had found... The one.

And she took such great pride in her ability to assess people. Because she did not feel that she was wide-eyed. She did not feel that she was naive. She had always felt that she was exceptionally realistic and pragmatic, and where had that gotten her?

Naked on a balcony.

Well, *nearly* naked.

And there was a man before her that called to fantasies that she had long tried to suppress.

He despised her. He did not love her as she had imagined Alex did.

And she did not love him.

But regardless, he had captivated her from the first moment she had seen him.

Alex had an ease about him, and Constantine was nothing like that. Constantine was every inch the man you might expect to have a mad wife in the attic. Constantine was...

"Do you think?" she asked, the question coming out much more breathless than she intended.

"I hate to see a woman all dressed up with nowhere to go."

His voice had become a seductive purr now, nothing like the interactions she'd had with him prior. His tone was usually hard, deep and clipped. And now it washed over her like a wave.

Leaving her feeling restless.

"You're very beautiful, Morgan."

He thought she was beautiful? She was pretty. She knew that, but it had always felt a little bit like an inconvenience more than anything else. Her flame red hair and translucent skin drew a lot of attention, as did the vividness of her green eyes, but for a woman who had always wanted to keep her head down and get on with school and work, it had felt an uneasy burden to bear.

She had never much cared whether or not a man thought she was beautiful, but for some reason the revelation that Constantine did was... Well it was heady indeed.

"You think I'm beautiful?"

"Yes. But I would bet you know you're beautiful."

"Perhaps. But I imagine you despise everything about me. I did not ever consider that you might apply any sort of virtue to me."

"Do you think beauty is a virtue?"

She blinked. "No. Not... That isn't what I meant."

"Beauty," he said, his voice hard, "is a vice. Were it not, I would have grabbed hold of you by now and shipped you straight out the bedroom door, flinging you to your ass out in the corridor. However. Your beauty is a particular vice of mine. When I find I am not a man given to questioning a gift when it shows up in my room trussed up and ready to be unwrapped."

"And if I don't want you?"

He stood slowly, never breaking eye contact with her, never wavering. Then he made his way to her, and she felt her breath go more and more shallow.

"Darling," he said. "Do not lie. It insults us

both. You have wanted me from the very moment you first set foot in my parents' house. And the more cruel I am to you, the more you seem to want it."

Her breathing was truly labored now, and she hated it. Mostly because he was right.

She could recall easily that first encounter they'd had six months ago. When he looked at her as if she was something vile that he had to scrape off the bottom of his shoe. And she had found him beautiful.

She had been thankful, then, for Alex and his easy charm. For the feeling she had for him. Because they had done something to shield her from the scalding heat that came from his older brother's disdainful gaze.

But there was nothing between them now. No feelings for Alex. Nothing.

"And you must know," he said. "How I have wanted you."

He did not grab her and haul her into his arms. Instead, he extended his hand, and with just the barest edge of his thumb he traced the line along the top of her cheekbone. And it was like a match, struck slowly and painfully before igniting the flame.

Her breasts felt painfully heavy, and she was so aware of what she was wearing.

"I knew you were beautiful," he said. "But I

was not prepared for a sight such as this. Even veiled, you're glorious—something to behold."

She did not know why it made her heart flutter so, because compliments about one's appearance were cheap and easy. And they shouldn't mean a thing. She had decided as a young girl to never let her head be swayed by such things. By romance and beautiful words.

But something twisted in her stomach then, hard and painful, and a voice inside of her spoke the shameful truth.

That she knew this wasn't romance. Or beautiful words, or anything quite so floral.

It was desire. And from the beginning there had never been anything she could do about it. Never been anything that she could do to minimize what she felt for him.

It simply was.

And, oh, how she wished it were not.

"Show me, Morgan," he said, his voice going rough. "Show me what I want to see."

He wanted her to strip. She understood that. She waited for him to sit back down, a king reclining, but he did not. Instead, he stood there, his gaze far too intense, far too intent. And he felt so large. He was broader and taller than his brother, by at least three inches.

And quite near to a foot taller than she was.

She ought to feel frail and shockingly vulnerable, and yet, she did not.

He had not an ounce of fat on his body. Not that she had seen his body, it was just that… Well she had been helpless to not take a visual tour of him anytime she had seen him in the family home. In his custom fitted suit that lovingly held his broad shoulders, muscular chest and slim waist.

And now, every ounce of his power, every ounce of his beauty was all directed at her. His gaze keen, his muscles bunched as if he were a predator ready to attack.

And she found that she did not fear it. Before she could decide what to do, before she could think it through, she reached around and unhooked the lace top. It went loose, and she pressed her hand over her breasts as it went slack. Her forearm neatly covering her from his view. She had certainly never done a striptease in her life. And it wasn't so much that she was being a tease now as she was feeling… Dazed. Wondering what the hell she was thinking.

A fantasy. He is a fantasy.

And should he not be the thing that you get on the way out the door?

Because it was always him, hadn't it been?

He was the one that had appealed to her in

this darkly sexual way that had always felt shameful to her.

She had always been so ashamed of this part of herself. The part of herself that didn't simply want sweet and wonderful words but wanted a man who wanted her. A man who would grab hold of her with big, strong hands. A man who would kiss her, taste her...

She had pushed all that down and told herself that she didn't need that sort of thing.

Because it kept her safe.

Because it felt like something that was too close to her mother and all of her vices.

There was that word again.

Vices.

Perhaps *beauty* was his. And *he* was hers.

And she would make herself a slave to it. For tonight. Just tonight.

It emboldened her, and she dropped her arm, letting the top fall free and expose her breasts to him.

His jaw went tight, a muscle jumping there, and arousal speared her between the thighs.

She had forgotten about Alex and whatever he was doing in the next room. Because one look from Constantine and her entire body was alight. And it had never been thus with Alex. Oh, she had thought him handsome. She had felt comfortable with the idea of sleeping with him. It would be no hardship.

But it had not been like this. This sickness. And perhaps that was one reason she had wanted Alex.

Because this was the very thing she had always feared. But the beautiful thing was she didn't like Constantine. So she would never be like her mother pining after a man far after he had moved on. She would never pine after Constantine.

She would heal from the disappointment of losing Alex.

Just like she would heal from missing the sheer sexual connection she felt right now with Constantine.

But at least she would never miss the man himself.

So her recovery would be quite a lot easier than it might've been otherwise.

"Stop," he said.

"What?" she asked, feeling confused now.

"Thinking. I do not need you to think. You simply need to feel."

She focused on the glide of the lace fabric against her skin as she began to tug the bodysuit down over her hips, exposing the rest of her body to his hungry gaze. She swished her hair and focused on the feeling of it skimming over her shoulders.

She felt the breath fill her lungs, felt her heart beating a hard and steady rhythm. Felt that place between her legs go liquid with longing, aching for his touch. For his possession.

And she didn't think. Not at all.

He appraised her openly, his gaze taking in the most intimate places on her body. He took a step toward her, and then moved to the side, around behind her. He put his hands on her shoulders, let them skim down her arms, and then he placed them on her hips and pulled her against him, and she felt the hard ridge of his desire pushing insistently against the curve of her buttocks. "I want you," he growled.

"Oh," she said.

"You are truly beautiful," he said.

"Now who's thinking too much," she said. She turned her head slightly, and then he kissed her, light, teasing. Not enough. She wiggled in his hold and turned toward him, and he deepened the kiss. And it was like fire.

His mouth was firm and hot, his tongue insistent and clever as he licked deeper and deeper into her mouth with each pass of his lips over hers.

She arched against him, completely naked, aware of the silken fabric of his shirt, of a button skimming over her nipple and making her gasp. She could feel the belt buckle on his pants pressing against her stomach, and beneath that the insistent evidence of his desire. He kissed her, and backed her against the wall, the plaster cool beneath her skin, with him hot and hard at her front. She clung to his shoulders as he kissed down her neck, to her collarbone, to her breast, where he took one distended bud into his mouth and sucked hard, making her cry out in a ragged gasp of joy.

She wanted him. And she was going to have him. Because tonight, she would not lose everything. She would not walk away a broken, demeaned woman who had been made a fool of.

She would embrace this darkest part of herself that she had always denied, and she would claim her power once and for all. She was tired of being afraid. She would not allow this to be a lesson in how she could not trust herself. It was other people she couldn't trust. She was not to blame. She wasn't.

And in Constantine's arms that felt true and possible and real.

Because he made her feel like she was everything. He made her feel like she was perfect. He growled, his hands hard on her hips as he thrust forward, making sure that she felt how much he desired her.

"I want you to know," he growled against her lips, grinding his hips against hers. "I do not behave in such a fashion. I like sophisticated women. Close to my age. With cultured experience. I do not like twenty-two-year-old waitresses with dangerous sexuality they do not know how to control."

And something in her sparked. She felt the corner of her mouth turn upward into a smile. "Stop then. If you don't like me. If you don't want me. Stop."

He cursed, something vile in Greek, and grabbed hold of her chin, his eyes meeting hers. "Little cat," he said. "I cannot walk away. Or I would have done so already."

"Then I suppose this is something you do now. You have painted me with quite the brush, Constantine, it is hardly fair that you get to excuse yourself, exclude yourself, from your own judgment by pretending that this is somehow an aberration, and therefore excusable. If I am an aberration, then perhaps it is because I am singular. A sea change in the world of the most immovable Kamaras."

"Then I will drown."

He kissed her again, and hauled her against his body, as he moved them across the vast chamber, toward his bed. He flung her down on the center of the mattress, and stood back, his eyes wild on hers as he undid the buttons on his shirt, as he stripped it off and let it fall to the floor, his pants and underwear following. And Morgan was faced with the sight of a naked man for the first time in her life. He was... Glorious. An Adonis carved from golden marble. Except he was not cold. He was hot. And that most masculine part of him was... Cruelly, dangerously beautiful. He made her ache with desire, even while she battled her virgin's nerves.

But there was something about the wildness in him that only increased her confidence. She was made to take him. She knew. Because he was made to need her. If it was deniable, then they would have denied it, that was the thing. That was the truth. If there was a way for the two of them to not want each other, then they simply wouldn't want each other.

Of that she was deeply certain.

He held her in no esteem whatsoever, and while she respected a great many things about him, she never wanted to sit down with him at a dinner party with only him as a conversation piece.

And so, this moment must be, as she had thought, singular. And inevitable. And that meant that she would take him. Yes. She would.

He joined her on the bed, but he was down at her feet. He kissed her ankle, her calf, the inside of her knee. And she began to tremble as she realized his intent. She had fantasized about this. Not him specifically, but only because she had gotten a handle on her fantasies in the last couple of years. Knowing that she needed to get through this last year of school, knowing that she couldn't go sleeping around for her own protection, she had done her best to banish her sexual desires. But there had been times... Late at night, when she had been unable to sleep that she had thought of a man, dark haired and intense, putting his head between her thighs and tasting her like she was the sweetest of desserts.

His breath was hot at the apex of her thighs, and she whimpered as he hovered there, glorious anticipation tightening her stomach into an impossible knot.

And then he took her, his lips and tongue slick and clever as he composed the symphony of desire that built to a crescendo, and then eased again, before finding its way to a crest, and waning into something slow and soft and steady.

Again and again he took her to that edge, again and again he took her there, but denied her the cymbal crash.

Again and again he made her mindless with desire as she twisted and writhed beneath him.

Constantine.

There was no doubt that it was him. For his mouth, the lyrics traced against her skin by his tongue, were wicked in a way that no other man's ever could be.

At least, wicked for her.

The most perfect expression of the rebellion that she had always tried to deny.

She was sobbing, begging as he took her to another swell in the masterpiece. "Please," she begged. "Please."

And finally, he gave her what she desired. He pushed two fingers inside of her, and the shock of the penetration sent her hips up off the bed. There was a slight stinging sensation, but her orgasm was hard on the heels of it, pulsing and demanding, drawing a scream up from her throat as her release went on and on, more than a cymbal crash, an entire finale with fireworks.

And she lay there gasping for air, barely able to move, completely unable to breathe. And she found herself staring up into his dark eyes, and she felt exposed just then.

Terrified.

Because in that moment he did not feel like a man she couldn't make conversation with at a dinner party. He felt like a man she could bare her entire soul to.

She felt as if he could see her. And for one fleeting moment she thought she might've seen him.

But then a veil was drawn back up and he was himself again. Hard and remote, but no less beautiful for it. She reached up and touched his face. Just as he positioned himself between her legs and thrust inside of her.

She gasped, and he groaned as he sank deep.

She felt like she couldn't breathe. Almost certain that she would be torn in two by the size of him. She was gasping, clinging to his shoulders for all that she was worth.

And then he began to move, the slick friction that she had found beneath his mouth and fingers returning, the pain beginning to ease.

She looked up at his beautiful face and saw that his eyes were clouded with pleasure. He had not noticed her moment of discomfort, and for that she was grateful. Because she did not want him to stop and ease her fears. Did not want him to stop and treat her like an inexperienced virgin.

She felt like a seductress in his arms and she did not want to lose that sense of power.

He gripped her hips and thrust into her with ferocity, the act of making love so much more physical, so much more feral than she had realized it would be.

Man and woman. Hardness and softness. The slick slide of their skin, the sensual overflow of his hardness inside of her. And with each thrust he carried her higher. Higher and higher. And when her pleasure broke, like a damn, spilling pleasure over her in a wave, his movements increased, until he shouted out his pleasure, the mountain fracturing above her, the shock of it sending her hurtling toward another release.

And afterwards she lay gasping and unbearably conscious of her nudity. Because it was done now. She had given herself to Constantine, and she had done it not simply out of duress or any kind of desire for revenge, but because she had wanted to. And there was no denying that.

"I will see you out," he said, moving away from her and getting out of the bed.

His broad, muscular back filled her vision, that sleek waist and muscular backside.

"Of course," he said. "I will get your clothes."

"Surely not *my* clothes." Alex's room could still be…occupied.

"Clothes that will be fitting." He dressed, methodically, and she felt slightly ashamed of watching him.

Then when he was finished, he left the room.

She crawled beneath the covers in his bed, feeling like it was the wrong thing to do. He'd taken her on the top of his bedspread, he had not allowed her to be underneath it, and it felt like perhaps an intimacy she should not have taken.

And because he was not there, she gave in to

her momentary desire to weep. Just a little bit. Just to let tears fall from her eyes enough to try and ease the pressure, around her tender heart.

He returned a moment later with clothes that were definitely not hers.

"Did you drive yourself?"

She shook her head. "I did a… A rideshare."

"That will not do. My driver will take you home."

"It's late…"

"It does not matter," he said. "My driver will take you home."

She got out of bed, and he turned around as she dressed in the clothes that he had brought her. "The car is ready," he said.

And then he walked her out of the bedroom, as if he were some sort of gentleman walking her to the door after a date.

She smiled weakly as he opened the entry, and she saw his sleek town car sitting there.

"Whatever business you decide to conclude with my brother or not, that is up to you. I will speak to no one about tonight."

"Thank you."

Preserving his pride as much as hers.

"Be safe."

"Right. Well. You too." She cringed as she said that as she got into the car and pressed her head against the cool glass window.

Tonight had been a spectacular failure.

She had lost Alex… And she had lost her mind.

She had given in and given herself to Constantine.

Except even as tears slipped down her cheeks, a slight smile curved her lips.

Because for just a moment, Morgan Stanfield had had a pure and perfect fantasy.

It was just a pity that it was over.

A knock woke Constantine around five a.m.

His first inclination was that it was her.

Her.

His stomach tightened viciously.

Morgan.

He should not have done that. He was a man who wasted little time regretting his actions. After all, what was the point. But Morgan…

"What?" He threw his covers off and went to the door, not bothering to cover himself before he opened it.

But it was not Morgan.

It was the family business manager.

And of course if there was urgent business it would be his door that the man knocked on. And not Constantine's father. His father was useless when it came to anything half so demanding as his business.

"Yes?"

"We had a call from the police," he said.

"What?"

"It is…" The older man's words became choked. "Alex. He was in an accident. He's dead."

CHAPTER TWO

"I DON'T BELIEVE IT." Morgan felt like she was made of stone, and she'd said these four words countless times in the past week. Now here she was, standing in the antechamber of the massive Kamaras home all in black, feeling faint.

She said it to herself. The staff was walking around brusquely, Alex's mother had taken to her bed, his father was in his study.

Constantine was...

As if her thoughts had conjured him he appeared, dressed all in black, as she was, his dark hair brushed back off his forehead, his eyes like chips of obsidian, glinting in the dim light.

"You came," he said.

"Of course."

"My parents will be glad."

"Will they?" She shifted where she stood, her heart beating so hard she was sure that he could hear it.

His lips shifted slightly. The ghost of a rueful smile. "As glad as they are of anything at the moment."

"You don't have to entertain me. I was ushered to the house, but I can go and join the rest of the funeral party out on the grounds…"

"Nonsense," he said, his voice hard. "You were my brother's girlfriend and he cared for you a great deal. Everyone knows that Alex never stayed with one woman for more than a night. And he was with you for six months."

"If he'd stayed with that last woman more than a night perhaps he'd still be here." She immediately regretted the venomous statement.

Alex was dead. She hardly needed to try to score points.

"You're not wrong," Constantine said, his mouth firming.

She took a deep breath and regretted it immediately because the air smelled of Constantine, and to her he smelled of sex. And it reminded her too much of that night.

His hands.

His mouth.

His body.

Him.

"My mother will wish for you to join us. To sit with the family. Come, have a drink."

Thinking of alcohol made her want to gag. She was already so unsteady the idea of adding a mood-altering substance to the mix didn't work for her.

"I'd rather have something soft, if you don't mind."

"A soda for the bartender?"

"I was a waitress at a bar," she said. "That isn't the same thing."

"All right."

He led the way, to a small—if you could call any room in the palatial home small—room off the main foyer, with dark wood and navy colored carpet. It was cozy, in a very old-fashioned interpretation of the masculine.

"This was once my grandfather's favorite room to occupy when he would come and visit from Greece."

"Did he visit often?" she asked.

"Yes."

"You were close with him. Alex mentioned that."

His eyes went cold. "Yes."

Of course he wouldn't want to talk about his grandfather. He was gone too. Just like Alex.

It made her heart squeeze tight. She wanted to go to him. Wanted to touch him.

The inclination made her breath catch. Hard.

She took a step away from him for good measure.

He went over to a wooden cabinet and opened

it, to reveal a small refrigerator inside. He took out a can of soda and poured it into a glass, over ice. When he handed it to her, their fingers brushed, and her whole body shivered.

His eyes met hers, just for a moment, and it was...

It was like being back there that night.

Had it only been last week?

Alex had been alive and she'd been so hurt by him.

But Constantine had been there and...

He was Constantine.

She could remember the first time she had ever seen him. So brooding and gorgeous and she couldn't explain the way he'd been beautiful to her, not when compared to Alex, who was so bright and sunny. But it had been different.

It hadn't been butterflies. It had been something darker. Grittier. A call to a part of her sensuality she'd tried to ignore.

But he'd woken it up.

Loud. Insistent.

He had ruined her.

Shredded her every belief about herself.

She had felt so confident in her stance on life. In her choices. She was better, smarter than her mother, who had made such bad decisions when it came to men. And Morgan had been certain she'd never do the same. That she'd never be derailed by something like that.

But she had been.

He'd touched her and all of her convictions had gone up in smoke.

He was her last remaining conviction.

It made her feel so small, but even now, even after everything...

She wanted him.

He did not step away from her. He stood there. So close she could breathe him in. So close it would be easy...so easy to reach out and touch him...

She suddenly felt lightheaded and she swayed in place, then put her glass down with a resounding click. She felt her feet go unsteady and he moved quickly, his hand going to her face, his arm curved around her waist, holding her upright.

His mouth was barely a whisper from hers and she thought her heart...

"Are you all right?" he asked.

"Yes." Of course he had only gone to her because he was worried she would fall.

Of course that was all.

Her whole body felt like it was on fire. And she wanted nothing more than to close the distance between them. To taste him again. She wanted it so much she could cry, and it made a mockery of everything she'd ever thought about herself.

That she was controlled.

That she was smarter than her mother.

Better than her mother.

No. She just hadn't met her weakness yet.

But here he was, dressed in a black suit.

Her sin nature incarnate.

She wiggled out of his hold because she needed sanity. She needed to breathe.

And just then, his mother and father walked in.

"I'm glad you're here, Morgan," his mother said, walking across the room to greet her with an air kiss to both cheeks.

Morgan felt scalded. Shamed.

"Of course," she said.

"Let us go and…honor him."

She looked up and her eyes met Constantine's, and the fire she saw there was black as night, and she feared if she looked at him for too long, it would burn her alive.

It was the graveside he could not stand.

This, he supposed, was the cost of having a family burial plot on the estate.

You had to bear witness to your brother being buried where you once played as children.

There was a memorial to Athena, but it was

different. They had not done this. Had not done graveside sadness and finality.

With her it was almost as if she could still be out there, even though he knew that was not the case.

There was no chance at believing in such things for Alex, though.

It was a heaviness that sat on his chest like a stone. And only Morgan, with her red hair stark against the gray clouds and the black coat she was wearing, provided any brightness.

"I thought I taught you better, boy."

His grandfather's voice sounded in his head—always in Greek.

I thought so too, Pappoús. But perhaps I am as I always was.

Weak.

Weak in his grief. Weak for her.

He was a man who prized control above all else. But what was the point of it? He could not control this. He had not. He had not saved Alex, any more than he had saved Athena.

He had all this power, all this money. He had not kept his family from tragedy, not again. Everything his grandfather had made him into in the aftermath of the kidnapping, of Athena's loss…

It had changed everything. They had been happy children. They'd had each other. He had loved his siblings. Had felt protective of them. Athena might have been his twin, but she'd been a few moments younger, and he'd felt like…

He had felt like he would conquer the world for her if necessary.

But then they'd been taken, and when her salvation had been tied to his strength, he had not proven strong enough.

When Constantine had been liberated from his kidnappers, it was not the miracle of that rescue that had shaped his life.

It was the guilt of Athena's loss.

The grief his parents had suffered.

This grief with biting teeth that had taken what was a chaotic, but happy family and turned small moments into battlegrounds he had not always been able to understand as a child. But he had felt the blows nonetheless.

They had not been able to look at him at first. For he and Athena had always been together, and sometimes he was certain they did not see him, but only the space where she should have stood beside him.

That was what he saw. So how could they not?

His parents…

They remained as ever. Fun and flighty, gregarious people, until tensions rose or anniversaries passed.

His birthday wasn't his own. On what should have been his and Athena's birthdays...he could remember there was no celebration anymore and he could never figure out if it was to mourn her or punish him.

He could remember hearing his parents once, in their study, on the night of his sixteenth birthday.

How different would it be if she had lived? If we still had her?

How different, he heard echo in his soul, if he had been the one to die instead.

They would avoid him for days.

Then his parents would compensate by buying him things. Cars, a private plane. And the cycle would begin again. This strange wheel of grief that spun ever on, a series of highs and lows, and always hoping they weren't crushed to death by it.

And he had his own anger.

That his parents had been consumed in themselves when their children were taken...

His parents were now all he had left, and it might not be an easy relationship, but in the cracks of it, there was love, even if there was also resentment, guilt, and he suspected a dark wish that their daughter had been the one to survive.

As for himself?

Constantine's life was nothing more than a series of complicated relationships and failed vows. It was in isolation that his weakness had been exposed. It was isolation that had led to his failure of Athena.

All he had been able to do was establish charities in her honor, try to find ways to protect other women in her name. So that her name mattered.

So that it lived on.

And he had sworn to live a life of certain isolation.

There was no love, no wife, no child, on any horizon in his future.

And this was another example of why. Yet again he had failed to protect someone who mattered.

Yet again, he had to swear to honor the legacy that Alex would not have the chance to build.

Though not just now.

Morgan was here.

And she made him burn.

One last time.

He would never see her again. She had been his brother's woman and she was only here now because to do anything other than pay her respects would be to needlessly uncover Alex's weaknesses.

He understood that without her having to say

it, because when his parents had spoken to him about including her as family, he'd not voiced an objection to it for the very same reason.

When the service ended, it was only himself, Morgan and his parents at the grave.

"Morgan," he said, keeping his voice even-keeled. "Would you like me to give you a ride home?"

She looked up at him, her gaze questioning. And then in a breath, he saw his answer.

She knew going with him was a mistake. He wasn't going to give her a ride home. Or, rather maybe he was. But he wasn't going to simply drop her and leave her. And this was something she knew, something she knew innately now because she'd crossed that threshold from innocent to woman who knew.

And she wasn't going to put a stop to it.

He did drive her home.

"My apartment is small," she said, as soon as they were out on the sidewalk.

But her words were cut off by his kiss. Hard and dark and she wanted to weep because this was what she'd needed all day.

This was somehow different than the first time they were together. They were both so raw.

And he was...

He was something else entirely.

There was no cool detachment, no control. None at all.

And she couldn't pretend it was an aberration because it was happening again. She couldn't pretend she'd make a better choice, a smarter choice next time.

Because next time was here, and she was diving in headfirst.

And she was afraid she might drown.

"Upstairs," she whispered, because they were dangerously close to getting indecent on the street, and there were still people milling around in spite of the cold.

The North End of Boston always had people out late nights, going to bars and Italian bakeries and pizzerias. She didn't need to put on a show.

"There isn't an elevator," she said when they went into the building and she started up the stairs.

He didn't pause, he simply followed her up the staircase and to her apartment door. She shoved her key in the lock and jiggled it until it opened. "It's a little tricky," she said.

She was embarrassed. She hadn't expected him to come over. She hadn't ever had a man over at all. Alex had picked her up, but never come in.

But he didn't seem to care about the size or state of the apartment. Instead, he was kissing

her again, walking her back to her tiny bedroom and smaller bed, and laying her down on
the narrow mattress.

She kissed him, arching her back against him
as he pushed his hand up beneath her dress.

Her mourning clothes.

This was wrong and she didn't care.

She wanted him.

And after tonight she would probably never
see him again.

She was being driven by grief, but also by
need. It had never been Alex for her, not like
this, something that had been made clear the
night she'd gone to Constantine's bed, and even
while she'd wept tears over the loss of Alex,
over the unfairness of his death. The cruelty of
a life that had burned so bright cut so awfully
short...

She had dreamed of Constantine. And the
guilt had mixed with hunger, deep down inside
her, and had created a monster that was raging
now, one she couldn't fight.

One she didn't want to fight.

Was that the same beast that drove Constantine now? Or were there other demons driving
him now?

For they were both kissing each other as if
hell was at their heels, and time was not on
their side.

Time was not on their side.

When this ended, so would they. And she knew it.

She knew it.

Tears tracked down her cheeks as he stripped them both of their clothes, and if he thought they were tears for Alex, that was okay with her.

He never had to know her tears were for the two of them.

When he was inside her, she clung to his shoulders. She held him while he trembled, as he split apart at the seams, raw and feral. As he claimed her, over and over again, sending them both to the heights.

She lost track of how many times.

He was like a man possessed, and she a woman possessed of him.

They had opened Pandora's box, and let the wave of darkness sweep over them both. Let it consume them.

When she finally slept, her face was wet with sweat and tears. And when she woke in the morning, he was gone.

And she cried like she would never, ever stop.

In the five months since Alex's funeral, since Constantine had left her apartment, everything had changed.

She had graduated—another milestone

missed by her mother, though there were so many it shouldn't surprise her. Graduation was one good thing she'd managed to do as she put her head down and pretended that the changes in her body were coincidence. Grief and stress.

But she knew it wasn't that.

Morgan needed to go and see a doctor. She knew it.

She knew she was pregnant because she was visibly pregnant. She needed to see a doctor. She probably needed to talk to Constantine.

But ever since…

Hideous grief and guilt assaulted her.

Alex.

Oh, the month after his death was a blur. Because she had never broken up with him. He had died that morning in an accident. Likely taking his lover back home. He had been driving his car too quickly, and had flipped it coming around the curve.

But he had been alone, and no one had known why he was out.

Sure he'd had some alcohol in his system, though barely above the legal limit. His parents had shrugged at that. A little bit of partying was hardly notable to them.

But they had not shrugged at the loss of him. Their grief had been a horrible thing to witness, and Morgan had felt absolutely bound to be part of it.

Because she had been his girlfriend, and they had not ended it… And… And she did care for them very much. She had worn black to the service, she had cried while holding his mother, sobs racking her thin frame.

And she had done her best to avoid Constantine's gaze through all of it.

That was when she had decided she had to get out of the Kamaras family's lives. Alex had betrayed her before he died, that much was true. But she couldn't tell his parents that. And if it ever came to light…

When she had found out she was pregnant, she was only more determined to stay away. Constantine didn't want her. What had happened between them wasn't romance. It had been an exorcism. And something beyond them both. It had been sharp and ugly, even as it had been beautiful. And she knew…she knew he would hate this. And added to that…

How would she ever explain it to Alex's parents? It would compound all the pain that they had been through that she had… That she had slept with Constantine. While she was still… She was still with Alex. It did not matter that he had been cheating on her, that she had decided to break it off, she had not done so yet.

And he had given her so much. That was where things like the gift of tuition, and all of the wonderful, glorious things he had showered on her during the time they were together began to model things.

Because surely she owed Alex more than he ever owed her. And now he was dead. And she mourned him, even these months later, even with the way he had betrayed her. Because in the end, she would look upon that relationship with… With joy. How could she look upon it with anything else?

And if nothing else, it had led to this.

Of course you don't feel an overwhelming sense of joy about this.

She looked down at the undeniable bump that seemed prouder than necessary.

Yeah. It was true. She wasn't feeling joy right at the moment. She was still in the throes of denial.

But she knew that… Once the baby was born…

No. She didn't know any of that. And she was terrified.

Because her mother had not been suffused with an injection of maternal joy and delight, so how could she count on the same?

They'd moved apartments all the time when she was a child, living in small, rundown studios, or sometimes with whatever man her mother was dating. Often her memories blurred, the settings amalgams of one another.

Whenever she pictured herself, it was sitting in the kitchen with yellow, flowered wallpaper, by herself.

She had one memory in particular of sitting there, kicking her feet against the legs of the chair in time to the clock on the wall.

She'd been invited to a birthday party. They were supposed to go to the zoo and Morgan had never been.

Her mother hadn't wanted to take her to buy a gift for her friend, so Morgan had walked to the corner store and used money she'd earned from watching her neighbor's cat while they were out of town and bought her friend a small off-brand doll. She'd wrapped it in tissue and waited for her mother to come home to drive her to her friend's house.

She hadn't come home.

Morgan had sat in that chair, hoping, until long after the party was over. And then she'd cried as she'd made her own dinner.

When her mother had finally come home Morgan had asked why she'd forgotten and her mother had yelled at her about how she'd taken an extra work shift, and she didn't need Morgan making her feel guilty about silly things when she was already overworked.

Morgan had been eight.

The thing that scared her the most was the way her mother was...no matter how many other men there were, she was obsessively angry at Morgan's father.

And while Morgan had her own issues with having a father she'd never met, who didn't want her...

She could remember the time her mother had looked at her and said: It's a shame. You have his eyes.

Like a failure or an accusation.

It was no accident Morgan had lost touch with her mom.

She'd visited at first, after she'd moved out. Then she'd turned those visits into phone calls that were less and less frequent. She'd made excuses about school. She'd called on her mom's birthday, Mother's Day, Christmas. That was all.

Then she'd started dating Alex.

"Sorry, Mom, school and... I have a new boyfriend so I'm just really busy."

Since Alex's death she hadn't called her mother once.

What if she was a bitter, distant mother just like her own?

Perhaps realizing that you could be, and deciding not to be, is the real answer.

Maybe. Maybe. But in the meantime… In the meantime she worried.

And she really did need to go to a doctor.

She also felt guilty living off what Alex had given her already, but she had been violently ill in the first stages of her pregnancy, and waiting tables had not been an option. Not anymore. So she had ensconced herself in her apartment, and had rarely left, only to get groceries.

She could get delivery, it was true, and right at first she had done that. But…

Eventually, she had realized that she had to get off the couch. Eventually, she realized that she had to venture out. She was having her weekly shopping trip now. Wearing the only pair of black leggings that she could fit herself into, rolled down beneath her stomach, and a white T-shirt.

She had thrown on a white baseball hat and a denim jacket, hands stuffed in her pockets as she strode down the street, eyes on her white tennis shoes, wondering why she had worn them, when she had to worry about the road grime getting on them.

She popped into her favorite bodega and got herself some milk, standing in front of the produce while she waited to see if a craving struck her. None did. She went to the freezer section and found herself putting ice cream in her cart. Then to the fridge where she grabbed cheese. And other than the crackers that she added later, she realized her little handcart was entirely dairy. And she would've felt shame if she weren't so blissfully, purely sorry for herself in the moment.

She suddenly had a strange sensation that she was being watched and looked over her shoulder to see two young girls staring at her. One had their phone slightly held raised like they were texting, but from a strange angle, and she had the strange feeling that they had taken her picture. But why would they do that?

She turned away, and then back again. And in a bid of strange paranoia she could not even quite understand, she put her sunglasses on. Then she got in line and paid for her things as quickly as possible, making her way back to her apartment. She spread her cheese out on the counter and chastised herself. She was being paranoid. And she really needed to get a hold of herself. There was no reason that anyone would know who she was. No reason they would be interested at all in her buying cheese.

Maybe they thought the guy running the counter was hot.

She thought about him. Tall and dark with an

easy smile. He was hot, she supposed. She had been burned by Constantine Kamaras, and she did not think she would recover soon from the scalding. It made any other man seem… Tepid.

She was just being paranoid. She repeated that to herself while she made herself a lovely cheese platter.

And she felt a little bit better about herself and her life, given that she had gone out, and now she had made herself a dinner that was actually quite lovely, even if it was a little bit sketchy when it came to nutrition.

She would be all right. She would not become her mother.

Of that she was determined.

This was her mess.

She would not punish a child with it for the rest of their lives.

And right then she determined that she wouldn't punish herself either.

CHAPTER THREE

"HAVE YOU SEEN THIS?"

Constantine's blood ran cold as his father shoved his phone into Constantine's face.

"'The Late Kamaras's Lover Tries to Hide Baby Bump at Store.'" His father looked jubilant.

And Constantine was frozen.

For a moment…

For one moment, he had seen her and he'd forgotten. Everything. That she had been Alex's. That she was not only his.

And he had…

For just a moment a sense of total possessiveness had drowned out everything. She was there, she was pregnant.

And that night of the funeral loomed large in his mind. His hands on her body. Her mouth on his. Being inside her.

The pleasure of touching Morgan the only thing that drowned out the pain.

But then he looked more closely at the photo.

The article had arrows drawn to each element of her outfit, proclaiming her a low-key style icon.

He had no idea what it meant. And had no idea why she was being hounded like that.

Except…

Alex had been a darling of the tabloid media. So it stood to reason that Morgan would be as well.

He took the phone from his father's hand and began to scroll through the article. It gave an explanation of the fairy-tale romance between Morgan and Alex, along with a recap of Alex's untimely death. It talked about how Morgan had been "underground" in the months since, and that this was clearly why. That she was trying to keep a low profile to protect the child she was carrying.

She looked to be quite advanced in her pregnancy. Much more than five months.

The child wasn't his.

The child was Alex's.

He wondered if she had been intending to tell Alex that night she had caught him with another woman.

And then he'd died.

She was carrying Alex's child.

And his father looked… Overjoyed.

It did not surprise Constantine in the least.

His parents had favored Alex so. He was like them. He was carefree and bright, and everyone loved them.

Much harder to love the one who kept things running. That had been his grandfather's function as well, until his death ten years ago. When Constantine had taken over everything Kamaras.

Because God knew Cosmo Kamaras, his father, could not be trusted to do it.

It wasn't that he was a bad man. Far from it. He was gregarious, happy, and often generous with his wealth. Much of the same way that Alex had been.

But he was… He was at his core selfish. Even if he meant no harm with it. His mother was the same way. Delia Kamaras was a rare beauty, the toast of any social scene she found herself in. She liked parties and glitter. Glamour.

She had much preferred going out to nights spent at home. And they had thrown themselves into that even more after the loss of Athena. It was not a mystery to him why. They looked at him and saw ghosts.

And growing up might have been lonely if not for…

If not for Alex.

And that was the essence of the issue with his family.

Feckless. Reckless.

And perfectly wonderful to be around.

But someone had to do the work.

And someone had to pay the price. Always.

Someone had to.

But a child from Alex...

"I have not told your mother yet," his father said. "She would be... Do you know what this means? A grandchild? What if it's a little boy? We must bring her here."

"Yes," Constantine agreed. Because regardless of his entanglement with Morgan, of course, they must have Alex's child.

It felt...

There had been a moment where he had thought only of himself. Of Morgan carrying his child. And that would have been...

He had vowed he never would. He would never be a father.

Ever.

But this chance...this chance to have a piece of Alex here with them. That healed something in him.

They would have more than a cold stone with his name carved on it.

They would have his child.

"She is poor," Cosmo said. "Perhaps we can offer her money to give us the child."

"I very much doubt that Morgan is going to allow you to fight for her baby."

"You are so certain? I thought you had absolutely no esteem for her. I thought you imagine her to be a gold digger."

His parents had instantly welcomed Morgan, but they were like that. It was part of their complicated nature. They were not cynical people. They had no real reserve, that was the issue. They said what they thought and sometimes they said things that were painful for Constantine. And sometimes they spoke nothing but love and support.

They had certainly done so for Morgan. They had defended her no matter how cautious Constantine was about her.

Yet again, he'd felt he had to protect Alex where they were not…

Where they were only focused on the good and the glittering.

"I did," he said, clipped. "She could've come demanding money from you at any point over the course of this pregnancy, and she has not, has she?" Of course, that wasn't the real reason that he didn't think Morgan would go after his family money. Or at least, that she wouldn't trade her child for it.

No. It had been the hurt when she had discovered Alex was being unfaithful to her. And the passionate way she had gone up in flames in his arms.

She was not a woman of cold, calculated intent. Of that he was certain.

He knew that now.

If he were bracingly honest with himself the heart of his issue with Morgan had been the fact that he wanted her, and she had belonged to Alex, and at the first moment the opportunity had been there…

He had wanted her. So he had taken her. And it enraged him that looking at her now, round with child, *not* his child, he felt the same sort of desire that had existed then. Only it felt feral now. Possessive.

As if it didn't before.

He gritted his teeth.

"You do present a good point. Perhaps she will consent to be part of the family. I don't see why not. Your mother… She was very fond of her. She was quite sad when Morgan faded out of our lives. It was so nice to see Alex as happy as he was with her. He was going to marry her."

Constantine wondered if that was true. He had no trouble believing that his brother could be unfaithful to the woman that he had wanted to marry, because Alex simply wouldn't think past the moment. He wouldn't take the emotion all that deep. It just wasn't in him.

At least it hadn't been.

He still found it very difficult to think of his brother in the past tense.

He wanted to rail at him. He had for these last five months. And now even more so.

You were going to be a father, you fool. Why did you need to drive that fast? Why did you need to drive drunk? Why could you not have settled? Why must you make me miss you like this? Why could you not have been more like me?

Athena had been taken, and nothing that had happened had been her choice. This was such a strange, complex pain. Alex had made his choices, and yet Constantine still felt he should have done something more.

And none of it fixed the hole inside of him. Not guilt, not anything.

Perhaps...

Perhaps this child would.

"I will go to her," Constantine said, on that he was clear. On that he was certain.

"Bring her here," his dad said. "And let her know that every offer is on the table. She's family now."

She's family now.

Those words rang sharply in his head as he

drove his sleek sports car down to Morgan's brownstone. A location he knew too well.

The sight of his last downfall with her.

She would have been carrying Alex's baby, even then.

She would have been the first time too.

The thought of it made his blood burn.

He went inside the building and made his way up the narrow staircase, confident he remembered the exact details of which unit she was in. He might have been addled by grief and desire, but he was not a man who forgot such things.

He found it quickly enough.

The security in this place was shameful. The floors and walls scarred by God knew what.

He did not want her living here, that was certain.

Even now, he did not want that.

He did something he was deeply unaccustomed to and knocked.

"Yes?"

The question was muted.

"Morgan," he said. "Open the door."

"You must have the wrong unit."

"We both know I don't."

"No, we don't know that."

Frustration rocked through his veins, but still, he could not hate her. "We do."

He did not know why she was bothering with

the pretense. He was a fool. But there was something so absurdly stubborn about this attempt at a charade, that he… Why was it always like this with her? Why could he never really quite hate her?

He had met her and they'd sparked off each other instantly.

"A bartender?"

"A waitress," she'd said. *"At a bar. It is different."*

"I imagine one makes it easier to meet rich men?"

"Are you accusing me of something?"

"Yes. Dating my brother for his money."

"I've only known you for a few minutes, but perhaps that is why women date you. Alex has a personality."

He'd grudgingly respected her then, even if he hadn't liked her being with his brother. But then, the real issue had been that he'd wanted her. From that moment.

"Maybe if you had your own dates at family functions you wouldn't be so concerned about me, Constantine."

"I don't date, Morgan."

"I wasn't aware you'd taken vows of celibacy."

His lips had curved and he'd had the strongest desire to see if he could make her blush.

If he could prove what he suspected. That she always ended up talking to him when she came to his parents' home because she couldn't stay away. Because of the heat between them.

"I never said I was celibate. I don't have to play games. Women don't come to me for dinner dates. They simply come for dessert."

"And the witty banter I assume," she'd said, but her voice had sounded tight.

"No, it's for the orgasms."

And he'd realized in that moment he'd overstepped because the air between them had become thick, and the spark had been palpable. And knowing? It had fixed nothing.

Even now he should hate her. He should be angry at her. For concealing this from his family. And he was. He was angry about a lot of things.

But there were moments where she glimmered, even behind a scratched up old door, and that was the thing about Morgan that made everything difficult.

"I'm not going to leave," he said. "I can tell you I could break down this door in a matter of seconds, and I don't think that anyone would help you. This apartment is appalling."

"It is actually very nice for this area and reasonably priced."

"How nice for it. But it is not secure enough to keep you safe."

"You aren't going to do anything to me, Constantine."

"Funny how you suddenly speak English. And know who I am."

The door suddenly cracked open. "What do you want?"

"I should think it's quite obvious. I am here to claim my brother's child."

Morgan stared out of the crack, the door opened as wide as it could with the chain still on, utterly dumbfounded by what Constantine had just said.

His brother's child.

But surely he knew...

She looked up at his face, and it was clear that he didn't know. "My parents are overjoyed," Constantine said. "So thrilled that Alex is to have a child. It does not matter what passed between us, Morgan. What matters is that you have given them hope. You have given them joy when I thought it would not be possible for them to ever experience it again. When my father saw the article..."

"An article?"

"It was in the tabloids just yesterday."

"It was not!"

"It was," he said.

"I didn't see it."

"Do you read tabloids?"

"Well no. But I would if I thought that I was going to be in them."

"Open the door, Morgan. I will show you."

"I am quite capable of doing an Internet search without your interference." She closed the door, then went and grabbed her phone off the couch and did a quick search for her own name.

And there it was. In the bodega. And of course the picture they used was the one after she had put her sunglasses on, which was when she had become paranoid. She hadn't gone out incognito, but they'd certainly made it sound like she had. Like she knew that she might be followed.

"Style icon…"

She zoomed in slightly on the photo, she supposed she did look quite cute. "This is very strange," she shouted back.

"Irregular," he said, as if agreeing. "Now open the door so that we might speak.

"Please come back with me," he said. "My mother has not been this happy since Alex died. You cannot take this from them."

Morgan hesitated, guilt turning through her. Constantine clearly had no idea that she'd been a virgin when they'd slept together. He thought this was Alex's child and… She had given him her virginity.

He'd been her first.

The only man she'd ever really wanted, and he had no idea. He had no real idea who she was at all.

How special their connection had been for her, and how unique it was. How it defied everything she'd ever known about herself before.

It doesn't matter what he thinks. He won't want the child. And maybe this is a way to…to give them some joy, while maintaining freedom.

It was clear that this was the narrative that Constantine wanted to believe.

Does it really surprise you?

No.

Because she knew how he felt about having children. A memory she'd buried because she couldn't bear to unspool it. And she'd become very, very good at denial these last months.

Doing her best to turn that hot, glorious night with Constantine into a gauzy blur even though she remembered it all far too clearly.

And all the days she'd spent at the Kamaras Estate during her time with Alex. It was strange how those memories centered on Constantine. They always had. It hadn't mattered that she wasn't supposed to be there for him. They'd always found each other. They'd always ended up talking.

It was like they'd been pulled together by forces stronger than themselves. Even when other people had been in the room, he was at the center of the memory.

"I personally will be an excellent father, as I am an expert in all of life's important skills. Drinking fine alcohol..." Alex had lifted his glass *"...driving fast cars and ensnaring the most beautiful women."*

He'd gestured to Morgan when he said that.

"And if you were to have a daughter?"

"I am equal opportunity, Morgan, perhaps my daughter will appreciate those skills? One never knows."

His eyes had shone with humor and Morgan's stomach had fluttered. Then Constantine had turned his dark eyes on her and her stomach had clamped down tight. She hadn't been able to breathe.

"A fine role model then," he'd said, his gaze flickering to his brother.

"And you, Constantine?" Alex had asked. *"What will you teach your children? To glower, isolate yourself for days at a time and miss the punchline of most jokes lobbed your way?"*

"A glower when pointed well is a useful tool. I think you mean work, not isolate, and if a joke

is poor, I do not laugh. Which could be why you never hear it, little brother. But I will never have children," he'd said, his tone definitive, *"so it does not matter either way if I have useful skills to pass on."*

"Never?" she asked.

She hadn't meant to ask. But she felt...sad hearing him say that. Constantine, for all that he perplexed her, bothered her, was one of the most beautiful men she'd ever seen. There was something magnetic about him. Something strong and infinitely...appealing.

The image of him holding a baby in his strong arms made her breath catch.

He looked at her and made her wish she hadn't spoken.

"Never."

And she stood there, grappling with herself. With how much of this was her looking for an easy way out of her connection with him, and how much was a genuine desire to not disappoint his parents.

And would he even believe her if she told him it was his?

Two nights, they'd been together. And even though they'd made love many times that last night... He must think she'd been with Alex countless times prior...

"What happens if I don't go with you?"

"I think you will find that it is a legal battle that you do not want," he said, his voice grim.

And that she knew to be true. Because she didn't have any power, not in the face of the Kamaras family. It wouldn't be a fight. Not at all. She might have been unburdened of her student loans, but that didn't mean that she was wealthy by any standards. She lived in this apartment, which was truly not childproof, and she...

She would just never be able to fight his family, she knew that.

And part of her...

A small part.

That girl sitting in the yellow wallpapered kitchen in the recesses of her memory, whispered: *And this way you won't be all alone, not anymore.*

Oh, she desperately didn't want to be so alone.

Did that make her weak?

Maybe.

But she was so tired of it. That was the hardest thing. She hadn't loved Alex. But being with him had given her a family, in a way. Even when she'd been sparring with Constantine at those gatherings, it had given her something. Connection.

With his loss, she had lost them.

"I will go with you."

She went to get her purse.

"Do you intend to open the door?"

No. Not until the very last minute. She didn't want to any sooner than she needed to.

She grabbed her bag, and opened the door, her heart thundering as she came face-to-face with him.

"I'm ready."

"Damn," he said, looking down at her. "When are you due?"

"I don't know," she said.

And that wasn't entirely true. Using the dates of her last period. And the date of their intercourse, she had calculated the due date on the Internet. But it wasn't confirmed by a doctor or anything.

And she should just tell him. But his denial in wanting children stuck in her mind, and it mixed with what she knew of her own father. And if she told him...

Would she end up alone? Would he react the same as he was now in his bid to...?

He was preserving Alex's memory, protecting Alex's legacy. If he thought the child was his...

If his parents thought she'd betrayed Alex, if Constantine didn't have that drive to protect Alex, then what would this mean?

Would her child be rejected, just like she'd been?

Are you worried about your child being rejected, or yourself?

She refused to think about it.

"Why do you not know?"

"I haven't gone to a doctor."

"You haven't been to a doctor. Dammit, Morgan. That is the first thing you will do."

"Wait a second," she said, feeling panicked. "You don't get to tell me what to do."

"I'm afraid that isn't true. You were behaving irresponsibly. By not telling my family about the child, by not ensuring that you've been cared for medically… Come with me."

She followed him down the stairs. "And I don't like you taking the stairs."

"I'm not a soap opera heroine," she said. "I'm not going to get shoved down them by an angry rival and lose the pregnancy."

But she put her hand on the bump protectively then, because as a flippant remark, it might have been humorous, but in reality it made her feel slightly paranoid. She had never ridden in Constantine's car. It was red and fast looking, and not at all what she had thought he would drive.

"This seems out of character," she said.

"What did you expect?"

She shrugged a shoulder. "A hearse?"

"As I said," he returned, teeth gritted. "We all have vices."

She was shocked to learn that fast cars were one of his.

"I hope you drive more carefully than Alex."

He looked at her, his dark gaze pointed, and she felt the full impact of him down to her toes. "I do everything more carefully than Alex does. Did."

She did not correct him on that. Because the fact of the matter was, he had not been careful when they'd had sex.

They had not used protection, something she hadn't realized until she'd missed her period. The entire night was such a blur that it had not sunk in. Maybe it never really would.

She still couldn't quite believe it was her life.

A Cinderella fantasy turned upside down. Prince Charming was nowhere in sight. She had Prince Brooding and a precarious fairy tale that could be broken as easily as a glass slipper. And still she wanted to cling to it, even as she knew she was doing something wrong.

But she was doing the wrong thing while doing some right things, and that had to count for something?

In some ways, she was protecting the baby, and Constantine, and his parents.

Still…

Bravery took hold just for a moment, and she got the courage to test it. To test him.

"Did you ever think that it might be your child?" she asked once they were driving down the road. "We didn't use condoms. We never even talked about it."

Her mouth was dry as she laid that out there. Seeing what he'd do, what he'd say. If he seized on it, or if he'd deny it.

He looked over at her. There was something dark radiating from him. The same emotion she'd sensed when he'd told her he'd never have children.

Never?

Never.

"No," he said. "You are far too advanced in your pregnancy for that."

She wasn't though. Whatever it looked like, she knew she wasn't.

"Are you an expert in the appearance of women during various gestational stages?"

"No," he said. "But I can see the obvious."

"Or is it just that you don't want to entertain the idea because it's inconvenient for you. Because then you have to admit that… That something happened between us. We both know that you were doing your best to pretend that was not the case."

It was dangerous to push him, and she knew it. And she didn't know why she was doing it. Didn't know what result she was after.

He didn't want a child.

She knew what it was to be an unwanted child.

And she would never…

She would never.

"What exactly would you like me to do? Did you wish me to grab you and kiss you at my brother's funeral while you played the grieving widow? You and I know the truth. That you were done with him, and rightly so. That he had betrayed you. We also know that we had an indiscretion. And I regret that. But none of it matters. Alex is gone, and he does not have the ability to defend himself or share his side of the story. His reputation is set in stone, and we are the keepers of it. The only way that it changes is if we tell stories about him, is that not so?"

"I… I suppose so."

"He cannot defend himself, nor can he make amends."

That seemed so entirely sad to her.

Because there was so much to love about Alex. He had made mistakes. A lot of them.

"A lot of people make mistakes," Constantine said, as if he could read her mind. Suddenly, the sound of the tires on the asphalt seemed almost deafening.

"The difference is that Alex's opportunity to atone for them has been taken from him. The difference is, that his mistake killed him. Without giving him a second chance."

"I'm so sorry…"

And it was true. She was sorry. Because he had been full of life and lovely, and even if she realized now that he was not the love of her life, she had loved him quite a bit.

"Tell me," Constantine said. "About how you met."

"You know how I met him."

"Yes, I know how you met him but only in the way that I allowed myself to hear the story. I assumed that you wanted him only for his money. But the fact that you did not come chasing after a paycheck for carrying his child when you absolutely could have… It has made me question things, and I would like to relearn your relationship with him."

"I really did just… I was so utterly charmed by him." She looked out the window and watched the city fly by. "How could I not be? He came to the bar, and he seemed so entirely out of place. His suit was so much more expensive and cut so much more nicely than anyone else's in there. But he wasn't a snob. He was gregarious, and he bought rounds of drinks for people. And when he complimented me, it didn't feel like he only wanted sex. It felt like he meant it. And I cannot tell you how… How rare that was. Men flirted with me all the time. Made overt passes, but it was different with him. He said he wanted to get to know me, and I swear to you that is what he did. He got to know me. He treated me with the utmost respect. He treated me as I had never been treated before. How could I be anything but in love with him?

"I didn't discover that he was… Alex Kamaras, *that* Alex Kamaras, for a couple of weeks. I'm not connected to the social scene, and I confess I didn't really know much of anything about him beyond seeing his name mentioned occasionally in entertainment round up articles. But I still wasn't familiar enough to actually understand who he was. And once I did… It kind of scared me. I'm just a normal girl. I never expected to meet someone like him."

It was true. All of it. But she left out the part where she came home to meet his family and met Constantine.

She had felt nothing but joyous warmth around Alex. And of course she thought he was handsome. He made her flutter when he smiled, he did that to every woman.

But she had met Constantine, and something had happened. Something she understood now was raw chemistry.

What was a crush with Alex, was utterly sexual with Constantine. And being a virgin, she had not fully understood that. And she had preferred the light happy feelings that she got from being near Alex.

"I find the story so hard to believe."

"I know you do. And I even understand why. It must be difficult. Feeling as if everybody wants to use you for your money and power."

She felt him go stiff beside her. It was as if a wall had been thrown up, and the emotion radiating from behind it was... It was intense.

"Yes. It is true. A family such as mine, older, carrying history that dates back as far as it does... We are targeted. The Kamaras family is nobility in Greece."

"Yes," she said. "I know. Because Alex took great delight in telling me that he was a count."

"Indeed."

"Though I imagine it's the billions that really causes problems, the title just seems decorative."

"In a fashion," he agreed.

"I know it sounds silly to say that I know what it feels like. But I do. You see, I have nothing. Nothing to offer any man except..."

"Your beauty."

She nodded. "Yes. I'm not rich, I'm not influential. I waited tables in a bar. And men saw me and thought that my body was a commodity.

That is all any of them wanted from me. And the first man to not simply want that was Alex."

"You know, he treated every other woman differently. He did simply want sex."

"Yes, and I'm beginning to think he perhaps had an entirely different… Maybe he was different with me than he was with everyone else. It's an attractive thing to tell myself anyway."

"It's true."

And it made her feel… She didn't really know. Happier, maybe. Or sadder. To know that the truth was she had been different for him. It was just that he had made a mistake.

Would she have forgiven him, if he had lived?

No. Not after what happened with Constantine. There was no question.

She would've lost him, more because of her own understanding about desire, than because of his betrayal.

They finally made their way to the grand estate outside the city that the Kamaras family lived at.

She had learned, from listening to conversations in the Kamaras household, that Constantine had his own residence in Boston, and also in New York, LA and Greece.

One thing she had never done was look him up on the Internet though, and she hadn't just to spite Constantine. Since he'd accused her of targeting his brother from the beginning, of knowing who he was and so she had vowed to herself she would never go searching for information about him or his family that wasn't given directly.

The magnificent manor house came into view, and her stomach fluttered. Or perhaps that was the baby kicking her. Which had become more and more common lately. As soon as Constantine pulled the car up to the front of the estate, the doors flew open. It wasn't the butler who greeted them, but Delia.

She had tears streaming down her face, and when Morgan got out of the car, the other woman flew across the empty space and hugged her. "Agape," she said, smoothing Morgan's hair back from her face. "Daughter. You have no idea how happy I am."

And Morgan's heart contracted in on itself.

Her own mother had never looked at her with this much joy. With this much excitement. With this much love.

No. Not even her own mother.

But Delia Kamaras was looking at her like she was miraculous.

And what would they think if she knew?

Yes, it would still be their grandchild, but it would not be a piece of their beloved Alex.

And they would know that she and Constantine…

"I didn't know what to do," she said.

Because that was true. She still didn't know what to do, but the choice had been taken away from her. And right then she knew that she could never lie directly to Alex's parents. She was going to have to figure out exactly how she was going to handle this. But she would not lie while she thought of it. "You will stay here," Delia said. "We will take care of you."

"My apartment is perfectly adequate," she said. "You really don't need…"

"It is not adequate," Constantine said. "Not in the least. It is dangerous, in my opinion, and not suitable for any child of the Kamarases."

"Of course not," Delia said, ushering her inside. "You will stay here. We will have servants at your beck and call. Food prepared for you. Everything handled. That is how the child of the Kamarases is treated, and it is how you will be treated. You will never have to lift a finger again. You… You are… An angel. Salvation. You are to be coddled and protected at all costs."

She looked over at Constantine, whose expression was something like thunder, but he did not speak.

"We will ready a suite for you. When are you due?"

"I…"

"She does not know," Constantine said. "She has not yet been to the doctor."

"Well that will not do," Delia said. "We will make a doctor's appointment for you immediately. And we will have him come here. And then you will let us know, because, we are about to leave. Our summer home in Saint-Tropez is waiting. And we of course never rest."

"Oh…"

"You will be cared for here. And we will of course be here for the child's birth."

She looked over at Constantine again, whose expression was utterly unreadable.

"Constantine can show you to your quarters."

Delia hugged her, and then fluttered off.

"My parents are very much cut from the same cloth as Alex."

"What does that mean?"

"They're thrilled you're here. They will see you want for nothing. But they will not interrupt their partying."

"Partying?"

"They are… Professional socialites. They do not work for the firm. That would allow them too much time to sit and think and they…prefer to run from their problems. Straight into bottles of alcohol and loud clubs." She knew what pain they'd suffered recently, but the way he'd said that…it sounded like there was more. But he moved on before she could marinate on that too much. "For my part, I run the business. That is something that I inherited directly from my grandfather. I oversee Kamaras Industries."

"I see."

"It does not run itself."

For the first time, she fully appreciated the difference between Alex and Constantine.

Constantine was continuing to make money. To keep the family business going.

His family… Spent it. No wonder he seemed different. More grounded. No wonder he seemed to carry a weight inside of him that the rest of them didn't.

She had been in the Kamaras family estate many times, the beautiful well-kept grounds and the stunning architecture both in and out never failing to amaze her. But she had never stayed here. Not overnight.

And now she was being shown to a bedroom that was personally hers. A horrible thought stole over her.

"I'm not being put in Alex's room."

He stopped. "No," he said, his voice hard. "You and I both know how inappropriate that would be."

"Yes," she said.

"Anyway, it is being preserved. My parents

do not want anything touched or moved. Understandable."

"Yes," she said, her voice hoarse. Choked.

"I loved my brother a great deal," Constantine said. "In spite of his shortcomings."

"Whether you believe it or not," she said, looking up at him. "I loved your brother a great deal."

"I do believe it. Now."

Tension seemed to stretch between them, an impossibly thick and difficult thing. It was nearly impossible to breathe. She struggled against the weight of it. And if Constantine struggled, he did not show it. She did not believe he was unaffected, and yet, he seemed to absorb the impact of all of it into his muscular body. Take it all on in a way that she just didn't know how to do. And that was when she suddenly felt angry. She was out of her depth. She had been from the moment she had met Constantine. She had never known how to be around him.

He had seemed as if he hated her and yet he always spent the evening talking to her. Even if his words were hard and sharp. And she had been hungry for every interaction.

She couldn't remember the point where she had begun to look forward to sparring with him more than she'd looked forward to seeing Alex.

She had never fully admitted that to herself. But she had always found Constantine. And she might have complained bitterly inside about how much he seemed to despise her, and still, she sought him out.

Every time.

As he did her.

This man who called to parts inside of her that she had wished might remain hidden.

Yes, there was Constantine. And he was...

He was impossible. Impossible for a woman like her. He could handle this, because he had bed partners before. Likely many, because he was beautiful as a fallen angel, and even if he was the more responsible of the brothers, the way he had made love to her...

The skill. Combined with the intensity of it all, it spoke to an experience that she never even wanted to achieve. It was a mess. All of it. And she was the one who would suffer for it. And she would never be free of them. Not ever.

She didn't know what would happen when the truth was revealed. If it would be. Or if Constantine's denial would smooth over reality. If she wanted it to.

What she wanted right now was a reprieve, even if it was temporary.

She didn't want to make the decision, that was the issue. If that made her cowardly, then right at the moment she would just have to accept that.

"Come," he said.

And she did, because she was out of energy. Unable to fight. Unable to… Anything.

They walked past his room, and her chest seized up, but then they kept on going. To a room that had ornately carved double doors. With flowers and fairies.

"What is this?"

"This is a very old estate, and at one time, the lady of the house kept this grand room for herself. No one in my family has ever used it. But my mother thought that it was interesting. So, she… Spent several years enhancing it."

He pushed the doors open, and what he revealed was… Stunning.

There were little paper butterflies and flowers all over the wall, a cascade of color that climbed up the ceiling and spread out to a glorious golden chandelier at its center. The bed was opulent, four posters with gauzy fabric wrapped around it. A gilded birdcage hung in the corner with…

"Are those doves?"

"Yes," he said. "My mother's pets. You may… Have them be homed if it does not please you for them to be in here."

"This is like a forest."

"That was the idea. A fairy wood, I believe."

"Well, it is that."

"My mother thought you would enjoy it."

Yet again she became completely overcome by the reality of the gulf between herself and the Kamarases, and she wondered how she had ever thought that she and Alex could... How they could ever meet.

And when she looked across the space between herself and Constantine, she at least had to congratulate herself on the good sense of knowing when they made love that it could only be temporary. Of knowing that the two of them could never, ever bridge the gulf between them. Because it was not simply that he was a wealthy man. A powerful man. There was more than that. He was Constantine Kamaras, and she was Morgan Stanfield. And they would never be on the same side of this unimaginable canyon. He would always be on one, and she always on the other.

And it only made her feel all the more isolated. All the more precarious.

"What is it?"

"Nothing. I just... I don't know how to be a person who might sleep in this room."

"It is simple. You need only to lie on the bed."

They stared at each other and sparks ignited between the two of them.

"I don't think it is that simple, Constantine."

"It matters not. The doctor will be here shortly to see you."

"The doctor. Wait a minute. Wait a minute. I have an apartment, I left all of my things and…"

"A member of staff has already been designated to handle the management of your belongings. But, I imagine you will not need many of them. We will provide you with whatever you need."

"I'm not… I'm not for sale, Constantine, you cannot simply… Pack me up in a bag and make me one of your belongings."

"Make no mistake, Morgan, you are not mine. But you are my family's. Take a rest. The doctor will be here shortly."

Then he turned and left her standing there in the opulent forest. And she could not escape the feeling that she was lost in the woods.

CHAPTER FOUR

WHEN THE DOCTOR ARRIVED, Constantine knew that he should let the man see to his business, but he could not help himself. He wished to be in the room. He wished to be there to hear everything. And he told himself it was a necessity. A responsibility. One that his parents had left to him. Along with the innumerable other responsibilities that fell in his lap.

The business, everything else.

But he just wanted to be there. That was the truth of it.

When he led the man up to the room, along with the nurse, and the ultrasound equipment, and knocked, it took a while for him to get a response.

And then when he did, desire was a living, growling beast inside of him. And he could not hide his reaction. Not even in front of the doctor.

Because when Morgan answered the door, she was bright red and scrubbed clean, as if she had been in a warm bath. And she was wearing nothing but a white robe.

When she saw him, her eyes widened. "Oh."

"The doctor's here," he said.

"All right." She blinked. "I see."

"Do not worry, child," the doctor said. "I have a great amount of experience with this. I was Delia's doctor when she had her children."

Which of course betrayed the doctor's advanced age. But, Constantine had thought that it was appropriate. To make sure that the heir of Alex had the exact same amount of preferential treatment as Alex had had. As Constantine himself had had.

"Oh. I see. Well…"

"We will begin with some simple questions."

Dr. Papasifakis had a gentle bedside manner, and as they all eased their way into the room, he could see that when Morgan looked at the doctor, she began to relax slightly.

"Go ahead and sit," Dr. Papasifakis said.

She did, in the lush, magenta chair in the corner, that was cast in gold like everything else in the ridiculous room.

And somehow, Morgan looked like a fairy in the surroundings. And it did not look ridiculous. He gritted his teeth and turned his attention to the doctor.

"And when was the date of your last menstrual cycle?"

Morgan gave it, and Constantine did his best to ignore the answers that she gave.

He let the dates, including the projected due date that the doctor mentioned, blur in his mind. He thought of Alex. Of all he was missing. That he was standing here when his brother should be. That he was doing all he could to honor his brother, to protect his legacy going forward.

It had to be that.

And then the doctor instructed her to lie down on the bed for the ultrasound.

"Could you…? Constantine…?"

"I will turn away," he said.

"I…"

"It is…" He bit back the scathing comment he was going to make about how he had already seen the whole of her, so there was no use being modest now. Nobody needed to know. And even as his body was gripped with the desire to see her, he turned away, while the doctor and the nurse readied her for the scan.

He heard the preparations, but he did not allow himself to look, instead he focused on one of the butterflies on the wall. A delicate, lavender colored paper creation. It was fragile, like Morgan. And far more intricate than he had ever truly noticed before. He did not spend a great deal of time in this room, or rather any. And so he had not realized how much detail had gone into each and every thing. Amazing, how you could see something hundreds of times, and never truly understand what it was you were looking at.

He thought again of Morgan, and his stomach went tight.

"Here we are," the doctor said, as a strange watery sound filled the room. Followed by a steady beat. "We have the heartbeat. And a boy."

"Oh," Morgan said, the sound fractured. And still, he did not turn.

A boy. A boy like Alex.

His mother and father would be thrilled.

"And here we have another heartbeat. And this one… A girl. A girl and a boy for you."

And everything inside of Constantine turned to ice. And this time, he did turn. "Twins?"

Twins.

Twins.

Everything in him went dark.

"Yes," Dr.Papasifakis said. "Twins. It is why she looked like she was at such an advanced gestational age. She is just barely five months along."

He looked down at her, at the exposed, pale skin of her stomach, that rounded bump. Two babies.

Five months.

"Five months," he said.

No. It could not be. Twins. That was a sick joke brought about by the universe. He did not want children, not ever.

Twins.

Alex had. He had wanted to be a father, and now he was gone, and these children were his last chance.

And if they were Alex's, they were, in many ways, Constantine's last chance for atonement.

If they were his?

Another sin.

No. It could not be.

He had spent two nights with her and, knowing Alex as he did, his brother had likely had her countless times.

The image of such a thing made his vision go black with rage.

She was his. She was his *and you were the one who took what wasn't yours.*

But they had to be Alex's. Alex needed this.

Perhaps you need it.

He hadn't protected Athena. And she was gone, there was no trace of her. His family had never even had a body to bury.

Now Alex was gone.

"Yes," the doctor confirmed. "What a great blessing this is for the Kamaras family. After all they have lost…" the doctor said. "And Alex. Such a blessing that he has two children to carry out his legacy in the world."

Two children. *Alex's children.*

Everyone needed them to be Alex's children. And yet…

"Thank you," Constantine said. "What must we know now that we are aware that it is twins? Is there anything…"

"Everything looks good. And she seems quite healthy. She is young and strong, and I have no reason to believe that she is at any great risk of anything. It is likely the children will deliver early. But that is to be expected with twins. And it is no cause for concern. We will just keep that in mind as we set expectations."

The doctor spoke as a man who had in excess of forty years' experience in the field, because he did. And Constantine knew that he should trust him, but he found himself seized by an inability to do so. Perhaps because he had lost even the ability to breathe.

And the suspicion that existed inside of him began to grow, and while he knew…

"What about a paternity test," Constantine said. "Simply for the formality of it all."

"Well, that we can't do until after the babies

are born. With multiples, you cannot take a risk like that."

"I see."

"But I imagine that is not a real concern of yours."

"Of course not," Constantine said, smiling. "The staff will show you out."

When the doctor left the room, Constantine turned to Morgan, who had wrapped her robe firmly around herself and was sitting on the edge of the bed.

"Did you know?"

"My due date? I suspected, yes. It is not a mystery to a woman when she had her last cycle, Constantine."

"Of course not. And yet you let me believe you were further advanced in the pregnancy than you are."

"I told you I had not been to a doctor. I also asked you if you were willing to entertain the idea that the child might be…"

"Children," he said.

"I didn't know that," she said. "Tell you the truth, I didn't know why I was so big. I just thought that it was perhaps how I was carrying them… Him… I didn't know."

"You have a history of twins in your family?"

"I don't know. My mother was always isolated

from her family, and I don't know my father at all. I don't know anything about myself, and this is… Driving that home. I underestimated… Everything. I underestimated everything."

"My parents need these children to be Alex's."

A tear tracked down her cheek. "I think *you* need these children to belong to Alex." She took a sharp breath. "After they are born we can do a paternity test if you need…"

"They are *his*," Constantine said, his voice hard. "There is next to no chance they wouldn't be, and they would be better for it."

She said nothing to that, her face going pale.

Surely she didn't *want* the children to be his?

Why should she want that?

Because Alex had betrayed her?

At least Alex had cared for her, in his fashion.

Constantine felt nothing. Nothing but a dark, bleeding intensity that had replaced his heart when he was eight years old.

That night, he went to his penthouse in the middle of the city, and he paced back and forth, thinking that he might find answers if he wore a long enough trail into the carpet.

He was not a man accustomed to indecision. It did not do to dwell on that which one could not change. A man was not defined by his good intentions. Nor was he defined by his beliefs if he did not act on them. One thing he knew to be true for certain. Morgan must become a Kamaras. Whatever the truth of the parentage of the babies in her womb…

Rage built inside of him, and he honestly could not say where it came from. It was primarily directed at the fact that the children might not be Alex's…

Or that they should be his.

Morgan was in shock for the rest of the evening. Two children. A boy and a girl. She was numb. She didn't know what to feel. She knew they were Constantine's babies, of course. And she should've just said something. Should've told him that… She should've told him the truth. Not that she had lied, it was only that she had not insisted that no test was needed.

What is it exactly you want? You want him to know without having to be told?

No. She wasn't that petty. It was just…

She was a burden. To her mother. She always had been.

But now she was having two children, and for the first time in so long…she wouldn't be alone.

It rocked her, to her core.

Two children.

And she should tell him. Flat out. She should

not ask him about possibilities or skirt the issue. But she was...

She was afraid, and it made no real sense.

It does. You are so afraid he'll reject you. Them.

He wanted the children to be Alex's so very much, and what if she told him and that loss—another loss for him—made him resent the children?

And she did not possess the ability to burden the Kamaras family financially. There was no way. Their pockets were far too deep. But it was still different than being chosen. Of course it was. She just felt like she would never be chosen.

And he was just so adamant they be his brother's.

I will never have children. Never.

She wondered why. And wondering about him felt so dangerous.

She was linked to him. Forever. Whether she wondered about him or not. The danger had already happened, in that sense.

The thought of it made her shiver.

By the time she went to sleep, her dreams were filled with images of him. Dark and brooding. Avenging.

But also the way he'd been as a lover.

No less dark or brooding, and there had been

something avenging about the way he'd thrust inside of her body, but he'd been...tender at moments. Intense, too. Rough.

He'd contained everything and given it all to her and the last five months without him had been torturous.

She woke up early and crying.

Wondering if the grief that had invaded her chest five months ago was really from the tragedy of the loss of a man like Alex, or if it was simply her personal grief over tasting Constantine once, and then never having him again.

There was a firm knock on the door and she sat upright in bed, even as the double doors to her fairy world opened wide.

And it was not a servant pushing a gilded tray into the improbable bedroom, no. It was Constantine.

Even at dawn he was in a dark suit.

Clean-shaven, perfectly put together.

The only indicator that all was not well was a faint shadow beneath his eyes. And she wondered...

She wondered if he'd slept at all.

"Good morning," he said.

Such a benign greeting didn't seem right coming from him. It made her laugh.

"What?" he asked, frowning.

"Sorry," she said. "You brought me breakfast and you said good morning. You seem almost human."

He straightened, his mouth firming into a grim line. "Do not make the mistake of thinking me human."

"You seemed like a man to me," she said, her throat going tight. "That night."

"Haven't you ever read mythology, Morgan? Even monsters can make love."

Her breath caught as she thought of him as he'd been that night. Strong and powerful above her, a bronzed god, powerful and dangerous.

Ruinous.

But he was not a monster. Of that she was certain.

Are you? Or do you just want it to be true.

She had never seen evidence that he was a monster. Ever.

He was firm, and he was…

He was something else entirely.

But he was not a monster.

He was not entirely mortal, either. Of that she was certain.

"I have come to a decision," he said.

Her breath caught and held. She wondered if he was going to acknowledge it. The children might be his.

They were his. She knew that. With certainty.

"We will be married," he said.

"What?"

"There is nothing else for it, Morgan. These children are part of my family. And they must be bound to the family in the name. There's no question that I will offer them my full protection."

"As their uncle? Or as their father?"

His jaw firmed. "I will make sure that they know about Alex. That they know who their father is."

"And if it's you?"

"It isn't."

"So certain?"

And she could see in the fathomless darkness of his eyes, that it wasn't certainty, it was pain. Pain and denial so desperate it made her chest ache. "What good does it do? Alex is gone. He has no other chance. I will be their protector. I will make sure that they understand where they come from. Alex was… He was a man with many faults. As you know. He betrayed you, and I do not take that lightly. But he was… In many ways, the best of us. He was funny, and he was…" He faltered. That mountain of a man. The first show of emotion she had ever seen in him.

Other than when he was inside you…

"I know," she said. Because she did.

Alex had been the sun. The entire sky lit up.

Handsome and glowing and far too much.

And she probably would've had a miserable life had she chosen to marry him.

Because like the sun, he could not be contained to one room. And he would've continued to shine himself down over all the land. Over everyone and everything.

He would never have committed himself solely to her, and that was what she wanted.

And she knew that Alex would never have meant to hurt her. He was not a cruel man. He was simply… As captivated by himself as everyone else was, when it came right down to it. She had found that to be part of his charm in many ways. He possessed absolutely no modesty, no humility of any kind, but it had all been expressed with such joy. At living.

And it really did feel wrong that he was gone.

But that didn't make the children in her womb any more his just because she also thought he was good.

But the way that Constantine seemed to need it. The way that he clung to it. As if he couldn't even acknowledge that their time together might've produced children…

He needed this. And she felt caught between impossible truths. Her need to let him know it had only been him. That it had only been him for her from the beginning, even though she'd been too cowardly to acknowledge it.

Her need to protect the babies, protect herself.

Her desperate need to both speak the truth and hide it.

Caught between fear and need.

"I'm not angry with him," she said. "For what happened. How can I be? In the end, how can I be?"

That much was true. If he had died while she was still in the throes of being in love with him, it would've been unbearable. But she had seen that she couldn't spend her life with him, and in that way... His betrayal had been a gift.

As to what else she had learned about herself that night... Well, that was where things became complicated. Because some of the lessons she had learned about herself were less than flattering. And they had almost certainly landed her in water that was too hot for her to handle. Because here she was, staring him down, staring down his marriage proposal...

Proposal. That was the wrong word.

It was a demand. Clearly.

"But you will not be a father figure to them, is that what you're telling me?"

"I will be their protector. And I will make sure they know..."

"Do I have a choice in this?" She wasn't a

fool. Constantine was a powerful man, and at the end of the day…

What she knew was that he actually had a lot more leverage than he was allowing himself to believe. He was a billionaire, he was… wealthy and titled on more than one continent and she was…

Up until recently a waitress. And everything she had was because of his family.

And if a DNA test was done it would prove that he was in fact the father of the children, and his leverage would only increase. As an uncle trying to gain custody of them, he would've had a challenge.

But she knew what he would discover if she took it too far.

She knew what would happen if she refused.

Because she knew that Constantine was the only man she had ever given her body to.

She knew that the children in her womb were his.

And she knew that resisting him was…

"My parents are overjoyed," he said. "And think of all that they will have if we marry. Alex's children. Family vacations. They will be able to watch them grow. Twins."

He said that last word softly, but there was a roughness to it that was strange.

"Why marriage? I… I can still go on vacations with you I…"

"What else do you have, Morgan? You have finished school, yes, but do you have a job?"

"No," she said, thinking of her hard-earned hospitality degree. She had left working at the bar when she had begun dating Alex and he had paid off her debts, and she hadn't gone back to work since she'd found out she was pregnant—she'd had enough savings.

For the future she had imagined herself as a manager of one of the nice, historic boutique hotels in Boston, or something similar. A high-paying job that allowed her to interact with people, earn a living and have independence. She had been so proud of the work she had put in to accomplish it, because no one had helped her. Until Alex. Alex had helped.

And where would that leave her dreams? Were they even her dreams if she didn't need them?

If she was financially cared for, what would she do? What did she even want? Especially with the impending arrival of the twins. The twins.

Twins.

It really was a lot to take in.

"You don't have a choice, Morgan. It was not a request."

She knew that. She knew that it was true. That he wasn't asking her for her hand, he was demanding it.

"When?"

"As soon as possible. You are already great with child, and it is better that we marry sooner than later."

"Of course."

"We will marry at the family estate."

"Well, that will be easy…"

"In Greece."

"Greece?"

"Yes."

"I don't even have a passport…"

"A small thing. And not an issue. I will get you the necessary paperwork you require immediately."

"You can't do that. Surely not even you can force the United States government to move at a speedy pace."

"I think, *agape*, that you will find I can do whatever it is I please. I am not a man of patience. I am not a man who waits. I am a man who gets things done.

"You will be my wife. And you will be my wife as quickly as possible."

"In Greece," she said.

"Yes."

He finally lifted the tray on the cart that he had

wheeled in, to reveal a mound of pastries. "Perhaps this will put you in a better frame of mind."

"Are you... Bribing me with butter?"

Her stomach growled when she looked down at the croissants.

"Yes," he said.

He might as well have said he was bribing her with sex. Honestly, both sounded good right now.

Looking at him made her ache. Even now.

Even now.

"But then," he said, thrusting a croissant her way. "You and I both know that I don't need to bribe you."

"Because the blackmail is unspoken?"

"Yes."

She thought of her own father, who didn't even know her. Who hadn't wanted her. He was willing to strong-arm her into marriage to keep the children close. But not because he wanted to be their father.

She couldn't quite figure out what he thought was happening. What he thought he was doing.

But there was something haunted and tortured in his dark eyes, and she could see it even as she hesitated to take the pastry from his hands.

"All right," she said. "We will be married."

"In name only," he said.

That hurt. Like a knife driven through her chest. Because she had given herself to him. Because she hadn't been able to control herself. Because she had wanted him more than she had ever wanted anyone or anything in her entire life, and he was easily making proclamations about how it could be nothing more than a marriage on paper.

You will have freedom. You have your children, and you will be provided for.

And she waited to feel something like elation, but she still felt like she was underwater. She still felt like she was in shock.

Because the one thing that she wanted, she couldn't give voice to. She couldn't allow herself to think. Because the one thing that she really wanted...

"Good," she said.

"Prepare yourself."

"How?" She took a bite of the croissant.

"Pack whatever it is you think you'll need."

"I don't have any of my own things."

"Then I will pack for you."

And she felt very much like this was a metaphor for her life now. Constantine was in charge. And she did not know what that made her. Did not know where that left her.

And she had never been simultaneously more excited or more terrified in her whole life.

CHAPTER FIVE

"I AM MARRYING HER."

"Are you?" his father asked, a chuckle in his voice.

"How else will we have the children in our family to our satisfaction?"

"I take it she did not wish to sell them."

"No, she did not," Constantine said.

And he bit back his commentary on the fact that not everyone saw children as tradable commodities. And not everyone prized a good time over their children, either.

Their recent behavior was triggered by the loss of Alex, he knew that. The increase again, in their partying.

They had changed their parenting after Athena's death. Their relationship to Alex especially standing as a testament to that.

However, when it came to Constantine...

He knew what they saw when they looked at him.

It was the same thing he saw when he looked at them.

Their failure.

Although, more and more, Constantine saw his own.

His grandfather had driven into him the need to change. To become harder. To distance himself from his parents and their hedonistic ways.

And he had tried.

His grandfather would likely tell him to feel no guilt or sorrow for Alex, since his excess was the cause of his death.

A man must have control at all times...

He had succeeded, until Morgan.

"She is beautiful," his father said. "It is not a bad idea to take her for your own. You shall enjoy having her in your bed, I should think. Keep her with us, we've lost enough. Let us keep the family together."

He gritted his teeth. "It is to be a marriage in name only. This is strictly for Alex, his legacy, his children." He would not touch her again.

Alex would have called him a martyr. And right then he felt like one. As if flames were burning him alive.

Was that the truth of it?

He had punished himself with a measure of isolation for the loss of Athena. Had promised himself he would not have certain things his sister would never grow up to have. Had wrapped it all in the harsh but necessary lessons his grandfather had given him.

But in the end perhaps what he really wanted was to make himself suffer for being the one to survive.

"Why must you be so exhaustively noble?" his father asked with a laugh. "You could do both. You could protect your brother's legacy, and taste of her beauty."

"Marriage does not appeal to me," he said. "Not in that sense."

"Marriage to the right woman can be wonderful," his father said.

"I prefer variety."

His father laughed. "Did anyone say you cannot have variety while married? It simply depends on the arrangements that you make with your wife."

He did not want to know about that either. What his parents did in their spare time was their business, and Constantine wished that it was never his.

"You will come from where you are vacationing to the wedding, I trust. We will be at the estate in Athens."

"If you wish."

"It is right," he said.

"Yes. We will be there. It is... It is appreciated, the way that you have cared for Alex in the aftermath of all this." As if Alex was still alive to be cared for. "There is still something of him to protect, and that is a gift."

But it felt like a commission being given. To continue to care for him even in his death. Something he could not do for Athena, who he had failed.

His father had said that to him once. Ragingly drunk and weeping bitterly. *"You should have protected her."*

Constantine had not shouted back, *"You should have protected us both."* But it had burned in him, and even still...

Even still he had felt his own failure.

After that his father and mother had gone away for weeks, partying their way through Europe.

Trying to forget the pain of Athena, and possibly the pain of what Cosmo had said to him. It was why, even though his relationship with them was difficult at times, he never hated them.

It all came from pain.

So much pain.

He never wanted to cause more.

Athena.

He had been meant to protect Athena.

He had failed.

And in that same way, he felt he had failed to

protect Alex. From himself, if nothing else. And then of course he had taken Alex's woman…

What if they are yours?

No. It was unacceptable. Unforgivable.

He had made his own vows. About what would not be his.

Love, marriage. Children.

Those were things Athena would never have. How could he have them?

And this marriage… It was different. It would be different.

"We will see you there," his father said, and he hung up the phone.

He was ready to leave, and he had not seen Morgan yet.

He stomped up the stairs and flung open the door to her bedroom.

She was standing there, holding a sundress up against her body, and he caught a glimpse of pale flesh. She was wearing a set of pale lilac underwear, and nothing more.

And he cursed the dress for providing such an effective shield for her.

"I'm getting dressed," she said.

"I'm ready to go," he said. "The car is waiting."

"I'm sorry. You didn't give me a time. You only said we were leaving this morning."

"The time is now."

"Can you turn around."

He found himself doing so obediently, and he heard the rustle of fabric, and when he turned again, she was wearing a white dress that barely came to her knees. Her red hair was like a coppery halo around her, and her curves were…

It was a strange thing, to find a pregnant woman so attractive. He would not say he had ever noticed such a thing being appealing to him sexually before. But she was. A fertility goddess, and he thought there could be nothing more appropriate than having her like this.

She looked like sex to him. All rounded curves and feminine glory.

He gritted his teeth.

In name only.

"Let's go."

They got into the car, both sitting in the back. "What about my things…"

"Everything is been sent ahead to the villa in Greece. You do not need anything."

"How convenient. Have you chosen my wedding dress as well?"

He looked at her. "Yes."

And he knew that it would be resplendent on her. He had simply asked the designer—a woman world-renowned—to make a gown fit for a goddess. And he knew that she would.

"And what will the world think, with you marrying your brother's girlfriend?"

"They will think what my parents think. That I am preserving Alex's legacy."

"Is it what you think?"

"Yes," he answered.

"It has nothing to do with the fact that you want me?"

"I wanted you," he said. "And I had you."

He could see the way that landed. Like a slap across her face, and he knew a moment's guilt for talking to her in such a manner.

She had been vulnerable and open when she had made love with him. And he could not accuse her of being manipulative in that way, not at all. She had simply... Wanted him. And had given herself to him with openness and sweetness. It had been the best sex of his life.

And he had told himself for a while it was because of the forbidden nature of it. He was not a man that indulged himself in the forbidden. Very few things were off-limits to him. He had money and power and women flung themselves his direction, and when he wished to do so he availed himself of their offerings. But Morgan had been off-limits. And that, he told himself, was why she was so delectable.

But he knew now it wasn't that. It was her.

And trying to reduce the thing that had transpired between them to something past tense and tawdry was... It was small of him, and he was not a man given to smallness.

"Well," she said. "How nice to be such an easy box on a checklist. Sex with Morgan. Done and dusted. Double check."

She was pushing him. As if they were back in his parents' study at one of their regular evenings, back before everything had fallen apart.

"I've no need to experience it again."

"Then you won't mind when I begin to take lovers of my own," she said, as the car carried them quickly down the highway toward the airport.

"Not at all," he said, rage building in his chest.

"I think I will enjoy that," she said. "I had of course imagined that I would be headed for a lifetime of monogamy when I met Alex, but things have changed. So maybe I will begin to sample freely. I didn't really experiment in college the way many do. Perhaps this is my moment."

"You can do whatever pleases you," he said, tension creeping up the back of his neck. "I am not your keeper."

"No. Clearly not. And obviously deeply unconcerned with what I might choose to do."

"And you with me, I imagine?"

"As you said," she pointed out, "even monsters make love. Feel free to spread it around the world. I'm sure you already have. I was nothing to you, after all. Just one more novelty for you to experience. And you've experienced it."

"Quite so," he said.

His private plane was waiting for them, and the driver pulled straight up to the steps.

"Oh," she said.

He laughed. "Did you think we would be flying commercial?"

"Well, I did imagine that you likely had first class…"

"I've never flown first class," he said. "I've never flown commercial."

"I've never flown," she said.

"Absurd, this, isn't it?" And he was struck by just how different their worlds were. And how little he knew of her.

It suddenly seemed not enough.

He wanted her. Desperately. All of her. The history of who she was.

Yet, she was not supposed to be his. Not in that sense.

"Yes. I would say that this is all patently absurd."

He walked behind her up the steps, and he regretted that, because when they got onto the plane, she stopped, turning her head to look around in broad movements, and he wished that he could see the expression on her face.

The plane was richly appointed, with a grand seating area with couches of plush leather, and a private bedroom and bathroom at the back.

"This is amazing," she said.

"Tell me," he said, putting his hand on her lower back and encouraging her to take a seat as he went over to the bar to pour her a glass of sparkling water. "Tell me why you have not been anywhere?"

They would have no attendant for this flight because he had wanted privacy, and he questioned that motivation now. His body went tight, and that told him exactly why he had wanted to be alone with her.

The very thought of it made the monster within him growl.

Possessively.

"Well, I've never had the chance to be anywhere but where I am. I grew up poor. And I got a combination of scholarships and loans to go to school. Alex paid those off. But before that, it was just… All I've done is go to school and work. All of my life. I've never done anything adventurous or fun."

It was a strange to look at her, and to understand. To look at her and feel…kinship. But he knew what it was to have a life consumed by responsibility, marked by a heavy weight, from the time he was a boy.

"What?"

She had looked very much like she wanted to say something, but hadn't.

"Until this. Until you, really."

She must mean until she had met Alex.

Because surely that was the beginning of her adventure.

A current of electricity arced between them, and he felt his desire for her growing.

"Don't look at me like that," she said.

"Like what?"

"You know like what. It's the way that you always looked at me, Constantine. From the moment that we met. I felt silly, I felt like it was just me. Until that night in your room… I thought it was only me. I thought I was crazy, and fashioning fantasies out of nothing. A girl who had read too many gothic novels and wanted to dance with darkness, rather than standing in the sun."

And her honesty shamed him. But then, what would the purpose be in lies? They could not hide their responses to each other.

"Tell me what you mean by that?"

"Surely you know."

"Surely I know what?"

"That I wanted you. From the first moment I saw you. And I felt so hideously guilty, because

Alex was beautiful and lovely and was so good to me. So very kind. And I wanted his brother. Who showed nothing but disinterest toward me from the moment we met. And why should I want you? Why should I have ever wanted you? And now you look at me like that now. Like a wolf who wants to eat me whole, when you know already that nothing good comes of it. When you told me that you already checked the box. Choose a story and go with that. But stop making things up. Stop making it confusing."

"You wanted me?" He did not know why that made him feel as if he had won a victory.

"Yes. Though, don't sound so triumphant about it. We all want things that are bad for us, don't we? It's human nature."

"So I am just human nature, and you are simply a box I needed to check. I'm glad that we had this conversation."

If nothing else, he was grateful that the moment had been fractured. Because otherwise…

He might've reached across the distance and taken her into his arms, and that was not a good beginning for their marriage in name only, he supposed.

"Yes," she said. "Wonderful."

They sat across from each other, he with whiskey, and her with sparkling water.

"I need to use a bathroom," she said softly.

"It's toward the back. You will find there is a shower and bath as well. You may avail yourself of the use of the facilities if need be."

"I might just do that," she said.

She vanished, and he took a moment to draw in a full breath, which he realized he had not done, not since they had entered the plane. What was it about her? He was a man of quite a bit of experience sexually. He should not be quite so tempted by this woman. This woman that he had already had. In truth, what he'd said should be accurate. He had her. And it should be done with.

Instead, his body growled with need.

She was pregnant with his brother's children. Twins.

A reminder.

Unless they are yours...

No. Fury fueled him. And he stood from where he sat on the plane, and he found himself stalking back toward the bedroom and bathroom.

He did not know what he was thinking. And that was a strange thing, because he always knew what he was thinking. He never had the luxury of being impulsive. Not until that night he had taken her in his arms and she had come into his bedroom.

Of course, it could be argued, that the impulsive choice had been made for him the moment she had stumbled in there wearing nothing but lingerie. Few men would've refused her.

No. He could not push it off like that. He could not make it as if he had not been a willing participant.

He gritted his teeth.

She was not in the bedroom. And he flung the bathroom door open, and she gasped, sinking down beneath the water, as if it could hide her pale, lovely curves.

His body got hard, and he stood there for a moment, and he was at a loss for what to say. He had done this, not knowing what he would do when he got there. And it was... Intoxicating. This moment of not knowing. When had he ever not known? He always knew. He was Constantine Kamaras. And he knew everything. Because he made it his business to know everything. He did not let other people handle things, he got them done. Because his family tripped about like they had no responsibilities, and someone had to shoulder it all. Because he knew that when things went badly, people died. Because he knew these things, he was never uncertain.

And he was torn between yelling at her, for what, he didn't know, and reaching down and lifting her up out of the tub and taking her into his arms. Flinging her down onto the bed and making her his again.

And he simply stood there. Inactive. And he despised it, because it reminded him of another time when he had not been active. A time when he'd been afraid.

She was only a woman. And he was not afraid.

"What are you doing?"

"Tell me," he said. "What is it you want?"

"I told you I'd…"

"No. What is it you want? From the world. From your life?"

"I don't know anymore," she said. "I do not even know what to hope for or what to ask for. I did not imagine this being my life."

And that, he imagined, was as honest as anything ever could be.

She had lost the man she thought she would be with, even before his death. Though he did wonder if Alex would have actually managed to talk her back around to being with him. He had been persuasive like that. But they would never know. Not now.

A beast growled inside of him. And he could not take his eyes off her.

Her breathing went shallow, her eyes dark. And then she braced her hands on either side of the tub and stood.

Water cascaded down her bare body, the glorious bump that housed those precious lives inside of her a site that he could not take his eyes away from.

His body throbbed with need. He moved to her then, quickly, and pressed her naked, wet body against his, kissing her, fierce and deep. She sighed, wrapping her arms around his neck, kissing him. He lifted her up out of the water and set her down onto the ground in front of him. She was petite, and he wanted to shield her. Protect her.

She made him want to rage at anything that might threaten to harm her. She made him want…

She made him want. In ways he had not, for a very long time. If ever.

His heart was pounding so hard he thought it might burst through the front of his chest. And then she placed one small delicate hand there, as if to soothe the raging inside of him, and it made him growl. He backed her up against the wall, kissing her neck, his hands moved over her slick curves, his need a living thing.

And then he swore, pulling away from her. "This is not to be," he said.

"Why not? You clearly still want me. You *want* me."

"What difference does it make?" he asked, his voice fractured.

"It could make all the difference if you would only let it."

"What do you want, Morgan?"

And he realized why he had come in and asked that question. Because he felt like she had come into his life, his world, perfectly ordered and controlled, always, and upended it. And he wanted to rage at her as if she was an uncaring goddess in the sky and ask her what the hell she wanted from him.

Why she had the audacity.

"I'm afraid I want the same thing you do. I'm just not as afraid to admit it."

"It is not to be."

"Fine," she said, and he felt her words hit him in the back as if she had thrown something. "But if this is your decision, then it's your decision. Marriage in name only. And we will take other lovers. And you will not touch me. But you cannot have me and others. You cannot give in to temptation and touch me, kiss me, and then fling recriminations my way, I will not live that way. You want me, or you don't. But you don't get the choice to have part of me. You don't get the choice to play games."

"I'm not the one who plays games. That was

Alex. And he is dead. I'm cleaning up his mess. As ever."

"How convenient. No acknowledgment of your own part in the mess. Of what the truth might actually be."

"We will land soon. I suggest you get dressed and get yourself together."

"Yes. I would hate for anything to look out of place. And that is, after all, your primary concern. How things look."

He left her then, heart raging, fury pouring through his veins, but it was at himself.

It would not happen again. He was not a man given to indecision, and yet, he had indulged in it. He would not do that again.

He refused.

She would be his wife.

And she would not be his.

She would be his wife, and he would not take her to his bed.

Because she was pregnant with his brother's children.

And they would never be his.

CHAPTER SIX

WHEN THEY LANDED in Greece it had been dark, and he had instructed her to try and sleep.

She had been given more milk and honey, and she had done her best. It surprised her that she had managed to sleep. Given the time change, and the fact that she was... She felt raw. Raw and endangered.

The way that he had kissed her, the way that he had held her... *And you tempted him to it.*

When she had looked at his eyes, she had seen that he wanted her. And there had been something so potent in that, because it teased the thing that she feared the most. Being unwanted. And in that moment she had felt... She had felt renewed. And she had wanted to make him prove just how much he wanted her, and she had done it.

Of course, the end result had been unsatisfying.

What did he want?

He had asked her that.

And she was afraid of the answer. Desperately.

When she woke the next morning, she took in the beauty of the villa for the first time. It was nearly palatial, made entirely of white marble. Everything was bright and airy, giving way to views of the Aegean Sea. It was a blue she'd never seen before. One photographs could never display.

The house itself was lovely, but it paled compared to the natural beauty that surrounded them.

She went out onto the balcony and stared out at the sea. It was silent except for the sound of the waves, the birds, the wind.

And for a moment, she simply stood there, soaking in the fact that she was in a different country. That she was living a life she would never have thought possible. That she was experiencing something wholly different than she had ever imagined she would or could.

And she tried to let that be enough.

Because the scary thing was when she thought about what she wanted…

Constantine was what she saw.

There was a brisk knock on the door and she knew immediately that it wasn't him.

"Come in."

She walked in from the balcony, wrapping

the white robe she was wearing more firmly around her.

"You must be the bride," the woman said.

"Yes. I am."

Though she could hardly believe it.

"I will be fitting you for your dress."

"I just woke up and…"

And in came a tray with tea and cakes. It was funny how he seemed to know that she had a strong preference for carbohydrates at the moment.

The woman began preparing her fitting station, and Morgan ate, drinking her tea and savoring the sweet tartness of the lemon cakes.

Then she found herself being swathed in beautiful, draping silk. A dress that did nothing to disguise her pregnancy, yet rather seemed to enhance it, and her curves. The straps went off the shoulder, the Grecian drape of the fabrics making her look like a statue, and it went around her stomach in such a fashion as to highlight it.

"It is as he asked for," the designer said. "And you look incredible. So bold."

She had to admit, it was quite bold. To wear white and highlight a pregnancy the entire world thought was another man's.

Of course, the truth was, she was much closer to being a bride who could wear white than even Constantine might think. Pregnancy not-withstanding.

She thought of him again, of that kiss, and she throbbed. She was no innocent. That was for certain. Not anymore.

She was far too well acquainted with what her body wanted.

But it was more than simply what her body wanted. She was more in tune with herself. Admitting it was Constantine she wanted, admitting it was him that she wanted, admitting it wasn't Alex, it had brought about a deeper honesty with herself.

She was hiding and she knew it.

Knew not outright telling him there was no chance the babies were Alex's was…

Protecting herself.

Yourself. Not your children. Yourself. Not him. Not really him.

"It is a good thing the wedding is to be this evening. Otherwise we might have to have another dress fitting between now and then. Pregnancy is so volatile."

"This evening?"

"Of course."

And after that, the whole day became a whirlwind. Her hair was fixed, her nails done, skincare treatments and peels applied. She was scrubbed and moisturized and buffed and masked and left glowing and tingling in the aftermath.

She hadn't even had a chance to look at herself in the mirror when she was bundled into a limousine and whisked down the side of the hill.

She didn't even know if she had a groom. She had not seen evidence that he existed the entire day.

The limo stopped in front of the church, perched on the edge of a rock, right on the sea.

"I don't…"

The doors opened, and a woman helped her from the car. "You are to come and stand here in the antechamber. And wait for the music."

"I…"

"My name is Agatha. I'm the wedding coordinator."

Wedding coordinator. So she was here at a wedding. And presumably the groom was somewhere.

She pinched herself.

"What did you do that for?" Agatha asked.

"Because the entire day is starting to feel like a strange fever dream."

"Well, considering I pulled the entire wedding together in less than two days, I'm inclined to agree."

But she wasn't the one marrying a man under

false pretenses, so Morgan didn't have a whole lot of sympathy for the other woman.

Maybe that wasn't fair.

And when the doors parted to reveal a cascading palace of flowers inside the sanctuary, she thought she really was being unfair to the other woman, who had clearly worked much harder than Morgan could've imagined.

It was... Astonishing.

Pale pink and lavender flowers were strung from the floor all the way to the very top of the rafters, it was as if the entire building had been reconstructed of them.

It made the bedroom she'd been installed in back in Boston pale in comparison. For this was something else entirely. This was... It was magnificent. A marvel.

And then she looked at the head of the altar, and she saw him.

There were spare few people in attendance, and she knew none of them.

She knew a momentary stab in her heart over the fact that her own mother was not here. And why would she ever be here? Her mother didn't care about a single thing she did. She hadn't even told her mother she was pregnant, much less that she was getting married.

She wondered if she would see it in the news. Her throat went tight with emotion, and she began to move down the aisle. And she focused on him. Because he was all there was. And it terrified her.

But it grounded her also. Because she knew she was marrying the father of her children. Even if he didn't.

You have to tell him.

Did she?

Yes. You're being a coward.

She was. She was being a coward. She wanted so much to be wanted and… She was playing a game. Seeing what would make him happier. She didn't want that icy, terrible look that he got on his face when she suggested the children might be his. And she felt filled with disquiet when he seemed to look at his own children as a mission of atonement, as he talked of telling them about their father. Their father was here. He lived. And he was a good man. A good man who deserved to know…

And of course his parents should know. They should know that they weren't Alex's children.

The ruse had never been to protect them. It had been to protect Morgan.

Because she didn't want them to be his responsibility in that way. Because she didn't want to be his grim responsibility in that way.

Because you want him to want you. That's what you want.

And she nearly burst into tears then and there because it was true.

She wanted him to care for her. She wanted the mountain to bend. She wanted him to look at her with more than desire. With more than that kind of angry need in his dark eyes. It wasn't Alex she had wanted to love her.

No. She would not let it be that. She would not let it be so intense.

And a tear did fall down her cheek then and there was nothing she could do to stop it. Because why was she really so sad? A girl desperately seeking love, and in such a silly place. From this man who didn't want children, from this man who didn't want her. At least not in any way that went beyond the sexual.

And at that point she had made it to the altar, and there was no more time to think about those things.

And so in her heart, when she spoke her vows, she did so with honesty.

Because she would forsake all others. Dammit, she would. Because she wanted him. Because actually, she wanted this.

It terrified her how much.

"With this ring," she said, her throat getting tight. "I take you as my husband."

And then it was time for them to kiss. And she didn't hesitate. She wrapped her arms around his neck and kissed him. And she knew that she had made a miscalculation, because the ripple that went through the room was palpable. It was clear, from the way she kissed him, that she was not simply grieving his brother. That she was not simply doing this for the sake of the children. Not in the way people thought.

And he would be angry. So for now, she would simply kiss him, because it was better than facing any of that anger.

But pushing him was the only way to get him to lose that control of his. It was the only way to shake him.

And when they parted, his expression was thunderous.

But he took her hand, and led her down the aisle, and out of the church to the same car that had brought her there.

"I think that was a bit much," he said.

"You kissed me back," she said.

The car began to carry them away from the church. "Where are we going?"

"We have a reception to get to, of course."

"Why bother with the show of a wedding?"

"Because we have an old family, because many in attendance are family, and I am making a show of this union."

"Yes. Clearly. And I made the wrong show of it, didn't I?"

"You did not make the right one, that is for certain."

"Yes, I feel terribly sorry for that."

"Somehow, I don't think you do."

"Well, you will have to survive the indignity."

The reception venue was a series of large tents out in an open field. And it was even more beautiful than the spectacle that had been inside the sanctuary. And there were more guests there than had been at the church.

"All business associates and extended family. Here in Greece, of course that number is legion."

"I see."

"And many of Alex's… Mourners."

"Ex-lovers, you mean?"

"In a fashion. He had many friends."

When they arrived, people stared at them. But Constantine held her hand and took her to a banquet table, where they sat next to one another. His parents sat down at the end of the table, and guilt lurched inside of her. She couldn't do this. She simply couldn't do it.

Not without telling him.

She had been wrapped in fear, so much fear it was hard to sort out exactly what scared her most. But she had to be better than that. Stronger. And she felt it now.

"Constantine…"

"Yes?"

"I have to tell you… I have to tell you. They're not Alex's children."

"I know you think they might not be…"

"No," she said, her voice growing stronger. "I know they are not."

"How is it you know that?"

"Because I never slept with Alex. Constantine, I was a virgin when I came to your bed."

A hush fell inside of him. She could be lying. But why? They were married already. It made no earthly sense for her to tell him this now.

The children were his. And she was his wife.

They were not Alex's.

She had never slept with Alex.

And of course all the world believed that the children were his brother's, because that was what had been reported. Because nobody knew that the two of them had ever been together. But apparently, he was the only one she had ever been with.

It seemed impossible. Almost laughably so.

"Do not lie to me."

"I'm not. But there was never space to tell you this definitively because…"

"Yes," he said. "Give me your excuses. For why you lied."

"You were in denial, and I didn't outright lie. You didn't use protection and you know it. I did suggest to you that they could be yours and…"

"You did not say they were."

"You said you didn't want children. Not ever."

"And I don't," he said.

"You didn't want to know, Constantine, admit it. You've been lost in this desperate idea that you were doing Alex a service and it made it all feel better to you, and I…part of me didn't want to take that away. Part of me was just afraid of the rejection…"

"If you are pregnant with my children…"

"You'll what? Marry me? You already have. It's only that I realize that I had to tell you the truth. I cannot allow you to spend their entire lives memorializing a man to them who was their uncle, certainly, and who I cared for a great deal, but who I never…"

"They're my children?"

"Yes," she said.

"My twins," he said, the words catching hard in his throat.

"Yes," she confirmed.

"A boy. And a girl."

"Yes," she said.

And then, without pausing to think, without pausing to do anything at all, he stood from the table, and picked her up, throwing her over his shoulder. "The festivities will have to continue without us. I am eager to claim my wedding night."

CHAPTER SEVEN

IT WAS FURY that drove him. That poured through his veins like fire. It was rage that fueled him now. He was beyond madness. Beyond reason. He was beyond anything.

His children. His. Morgan was pregnant with his children.

She had never been with his brother.

She had been a virgin when she had come into his bed.

Everything in him roared.

He couldn't see the guests. His parents. Anyone. And he didn't care to. All he cared about was the need that fired through his veins. The reckless, raging desire that drove him now.

Morgan said nothing. She simply hung over his shoulder, as if in shock, and he strode toward his car.

"We won't be needing a driver," he said, and then he put her in the passenger seat, and commandeered the driver spot.

"Constantine…"

"Yes?" he said.

"I didn't know how to handle this. And I'm sorry. I get the sense that you…"

"They are mine," he said. "And you are mine."

"Yes," she said.

And it was all he needed to hear.

He drove away from the venue, the tires squealing on the asphalt as he did. Only he didn't drive back to the estate.

"Where are we going?"

"Somewhere else." He needed to take her away. And he knew exactly where.

He pushed a button on the dash of the car. "Have the boat prepared."

"A boat?"

He would take her to the island. And there… There they could sort this out. There, they would get to the truth of it.

But first…

First, he had his wedding night claim.

"We have a lot of talking to do."

"You didn't listen," she said. "I did ask you…"

"You did ask me if I had entertained the idea that they might be mine. What you did not say was that you definitively knew. That you were a virgin, who had never been with a man before coming to my bed. Isn't that true?"

"It is a hypocrisy to be so angry at me."

"You could've cleared all of it up. There were talks of paternity tests that we could not get because they were twins. *Twins.*"

"I knew we didn't need a test. I let you talk, yes. But you wanted the story, Constantine. You wanted the lie."

It hit him hard. Bitterly so, because what she said was true. "It would have been better if it were the truth."

"And I know you felt that way, so why would I feel… I was afraid. I knew it would hurt your parents, and I knew it would hurt you. I knew it would…hurt me. To be in this conversation. To feel the sting of your rejection. I knew. So yes, I didn't come out and say it. But you must understand why."

"I…"

"Is it so hard for you to bend?"

He didn't understand bending. Only standing tall or breaking. And he refused to break.

"Yes," he said, his voice rough. "It is impossible."

"An acknowledgment of the truth doesn't have to be bending. It can just look like acceptance. Or so I am learning."

He paused for a long moment. "I am well aware of the fact fantasy serves no purpose. I am a believer in reality. I…thought. You are right. The force of my…"

"You can say it's denial."

"I don't want to."

"Oh. Well. Denial about your denial—that really is something."

"*Twins*, Morgan."

"No one is more surprised about that than I am," she said.

"I'm not surprised," he said. "I wish I could be. And I know that... I know that this is another part of why I...why I could not entertain the idea that they belonged to me."

"Why aren't you surprised?"

"Did no one tell you, *agape*? I am a twin."

Her eyes went wide, and she turned her head sharply. "I didn't know that."

"You really had no designs on his money, did you?"

"No. I told you that. I really didn't know who he was when I first met him in the bar. I thought he was outrageously handsome and I was charmed by the fact that he didn't immediately try to sleep with me. And even after he'd gone out with me a couple of times, when I told him that I was a virgin he... He seemed to respect the fact that there were reasons I had not... This isn't about me. I did not know you were a twin."

"I was," he said, and he determined that he would not be speaking about Athena. Not now.

"I'm sorry…"

"Now you will tell me about you," he said.

"You know about me."

"Apparently I do not."

He'd called it a boat, but it was a yacht. A sleek vessel fashioned to look like it was moving fast, even while moored in the harbor.

"I've never been out on a boat before." She looked pale and wide-eyed and he was regretful of that.

He had frightened her.

He did not wish to frighten her. He was driven now by the need to get her away from here. By the need to have her to himself.

"I have medication for seasickness on board." His gut went tight. "I do hope you won't find yourself indisposed."

Because tonight… Tonight he would have her. And tomorrow they would speak. There were many things to discuss. But tonight, she would be his.

"Who's going to handle your car…"

"It will be handled."

"I have no idea what that must be like. To just trust that all the details will come together the way that you wish them to. I've never been able to bank on that. And I hope… I hope that you can understand that. I hope that you can understand that in my world things don't just work out. And when I found out that I was pregnant…"

"You think that things in my world simply work out? No. What I have is money and a staff that know exactly how I want things. And if I am taking myself to the boat, that I will obviously need something to be done with my car. It will be handled, because I hire people who think in that fashion. But that does not mean the broader world bends itself to my will. My brother is dead." He could feel himself beginning to break apart. This reality was so bleak, and he would have never said he was a man who clung to fairy tales, but he could see now… he did have them. He did cling to things. "And how do you think that affects me?" he asked, his voice sounding as broken as his soul.

"I…"

"I *was* a twin," he said. "I am no longer." It was only him now. Him, his parents. These children. The children she carried. "So you tell me, how is it that you think the world bends to my will? How is it that you think everything works out for me? Whenever I can wield my power and money, I do. But I do not control the whims of fate. I cannot stay the hand of bloodthirsty men, and I cannot stop… I cannot stop my idiot younger brother from taking a turn too fast. There are great many things I cannot control.

With you, *agape*. You are mine. And this boat, is private. Both of those things, are certainties."

He was in desperate need of certainty. Something to hold on to.

The back of the vessel was wide and flat, with a large lounge—big enough for at least ten people—and pillows on a raised platform. Morgan went and took a seat in the center of it, pale in her wedding gown, the silken fabric spread out around her. Like a selkie who had escaped the water and found a soft respite.

He turned away from her.

He unmoored the boat, and then took his position at the wheel, maneuvering them out of the harbor. Once they were in open water, he charted the course for the island, and turned on the autopilot.

He walked to the back of the yacht and stood, looking down at her.

"I'm sorry," she said. "I spoke out of turn. Shouldn't have said that about your brother. About you."

"It is no matter. I'm not sensitive. I have dealt with real struggle, and money makes a great deal of things easier. Both of those things are true."

"I have mostly thought about myself," she said. "Through all of this. I'm sorry. I didn't give enough weight to your loss, and I'm sorry."

A bleakness washed itself over him. His children.

The fierce possessiveness that had risen up when he'd made that realization had quieted some now.

But this was not a chance of atonement. It was simply evidence of another sin.

And he would've married her regardless. He would be here, regardless. Because he would not compound one sin with another. He would not leave his own children without a father simply because…

Simply because he had vowed not to have them.

It was too late for that. He had taken his brother's woman in a moment of weakness, and now he had even stripped Alex of his legacy.

No. It wasn't that you took anything from him. She was never with him.

She was his.

"Why were you a virgin?"

She laughed. "What a question. You said we would talk tomorrow."

"I did. But I have things we must discuss before."

Heat streaked through him like a lightning bolt. And she understood. He could see when she did.

She looked away, her cheeks turning red.

"Why were you a virgin?"

"I was afraid of this," she said, putting her hand on her stomach. "Desperately. All of my life. My mother was young, barely out of high school, and my father got her pregnant. He wanted nothing to do with me. He left, and she could never even find him. She never got a cent of child support, she spent my entire childhood talking about how much easier her life would have been if not for me. About how she regretted ever meeting my father. She was bitter. She said raising me ruined her dreams."

"No," he said, anger welling in his chest. "She ruined her own dreams. People are in charge of their own actions, and perhaps they have unforeseen effects. It does not matter, though. What your father did, that was his fault. His sin. But she could have given you up for adoption, perhaps that wouldn't have been easy either, but it would have solved the issue of her resenting you. She didn't make that decision. She chose to keep you with her, and she chose to live in that resentment. That was her own decision."

"What would you know about that, considering you're a man who didn't even want children. How can you say what my mother should've done?"

"I'm a man who owns his decisions."

"That's a lie. You were ready to pretend that there was no way these children could be yours."

"I assumed," he said. "That you had been in my brother's bed for months. I assumed that the likelihood that it was his seed that had taken root inside of your womb was much higher than the reality of my own doing the same."

"Well. Now you know. Now you know the truth of it."

"You were going to sleep with Alex that night," he said.

She nodded. "I was ready. I trusted him."

And something inside of him broke. Because he had not known how vulnerable a place Morgan was in when she had come to his bed. He had thought that he had been looking at an entirely different situation than the one he was.

She had been a virgin. Heartbroken because her instincts had been so very wrong.

"He must've loved you, though," he said. "To not sleep with you. To want you in his life anyway."

"That's a terrible thing," Morgan said. "I think he did. But in the end of it all, I don't think I loved him. I think I didn't know what love was. He was handsome, and he turned my head. And he was kind to me. And no, I wasn't interested in his money in the beginning, but I really appreciated how much easier my life was with it. I was tired. I was tired of the person I had the strongest connection to—my mother—resenting me. I was tired of working so hard. And suddenly, I had Alex. And he was fun and wonderful. He made me laugh. He made me feel like I wasn't a burden. He gave gifts to me happily. And I... If that's what being a gold digger is, I suppose I actually am one. Because I met you, Constantine, and I knew that it wasn't really Alex's bed I wanted to be in. I wanted to want him. And he was easy to feel an attraction to. But it wasn't the same. It never was."

She was so brave in this moment it shamed him.

It made him want to be more for her.

He stepped down to where she sat and gripping her chin, tilted her face up at his. "Tell me more about how you want me."

She was pregnant with his children. And there were serious things to deal with. There was outrage, and a fair amount of recrimination for the universe. But... It would wait. It would wait until this was through. It would wait until he was finished with her.

"Your intensity. I... The moment I saw you..."

"You know why I hated you so, Morgan?"

She shook her head.

"Because the only time I have ever wanted anything in the universe that I could not have was when a person died. When they were taken from me by forces much more powerful than I could ever be. But you… You were there. Flesh and blood in the most beautiful woman I had ever seen. And you were his. Alex is my younger brother, and he is… He was… So full of life, and I… I pledged to care for him. To look out for him. And I coveted his woman beyond all else. And I despised you for it. Because from the moment I first saw you I wanted you beyond all else."

"Why?" There was something hungry in the question. Greedy. And his body responded to it. He wanted to satiate it. That question. That raw need in her eyes.

"Maybe your beauty. Perhaps your innocence."

"You knew I was innocent."

"No. And I did not properly get to enjoy it. Tell me, had you ever seen a naked man?"

"No," she whispered. "Only you."

The monster within him gloried in that answer.

"Have you ever taken a man into your mouth?"

She shook her head. "No."

And all these months he had been tortured by the image of her pleasuring his brother, his brother having the thing that he could not, and in fact, she had never given herself to Alex. Only to Constantine. And the guilt that came along with the triumph of it all stunned him.

The water around them was clear, glimmering bright in the sun. And he had the desperate urge to see her body, bare beneath the sky. With no secrets. No lies.

He took her hand and had her stand, then reached around and pulled the zipper tab on her dress, drawing it down her body. It fell slack, revealing her pale, glimmering curves. She had on a pair of white panties beneath the dress, no bra. His need for her was a beast. Those curves—always so tempting to him—enhanced now by her pregnancy.

His children.

A surge of possessiveness went through him and he dropped to his knees, putting his hand on her stomach, desire and pure, masculine pride vying for pride of place.

He pressed his lips to her stomach and felt her shiver. Then he moved lower, gripping her underwear and drawing them down her thighs, leaning in and pressing his face to the cleft there, inhaling the scent of her arousal.

She was wearing heels now, and nothing more. And he had never seen anything more beautiful in his life.

Morgan. His.

No one else's.

Not ever.

His children.

And he knew then that he would die for them. For her. He would also kill for them. For her.

Self-sacrifice and violence were armor that he put over himself just then. The truth, a reality as incontrovertible as if the items had been forged in the fire, and not simply in the intensity of his own need to keep the world at bay.

Because he would not lose them. He would lose nothing. Not anymore. Never again.

Never again.

And this was what he had tried to avoid for all of these years. And this was why he had vowed that he would never...

This was why.

Because there was no certainty here. There was nothing but the vast stretch of terror that was the universe, that was fate. For he had not lied when he said that to her.

He had no illusions that he was all-powerful. He never had.

He had no illusions that things would be all right, because they often were not.

And what he'd said about her mother was true as well. He was a man who owned his choices. He had made the wrong choices.

He had failed.

And he accepted that punishment as his.

You even failed at punishing yourself. Here she is. In your arms. Pregnant.

And he pushed all that aside, because now, right now, he was going to seize it. Right now, she would be his. Right now, this reality was his, and he would not let guilt or doubt or recrimination creep in. This was what happened, and he could not rail at it any more than he could rail at the fact that he was the last remaining of his siblings.

It was simply what was.

And he let everything go. Everything except the dark need to possess her. Everything.

He looked at her. Ate into her with a dark need that had taken over everything.

She gasped, and he clung to her, his hands splayed over the globes of her buttocks as he licked deeper and deeper between her thighs, as he made her tremble, shake and moan.

No man had ever done this for her. Only he had tasted this honey delight between her legs.

And only he ever would. No man would ever touch her. There was to be no marriage on paper. This was a marriage between their bodies. They were joined together in this desire. In this truth that she belonged to only him. She was his.

She was his.

The sun shone high above, the open sky watching.

Do you see? He asked the powers that be. *Do you see that she is mine. She is mine, and you will not come for her.*

He laid her down on the deck of the boat, knowing that it was hard, knowing that he should take her down to the bed. That he should lay her on soft sheets.

But there was nothing but heat now, no consideration for comfort.

He stripped his clothes from his body, pressing his palms down to her knees and spreading her legs wide, taking a long, leisurely look at her. Every inch of her.

Her breasts were pale, tipped with light pink crests that made his mouth water. That place between her thighs was the color of strawberries and cream, and he knew it tasted just as good.

Her fiery hair fanned out around her, and she looked delicate, innocent and carnal all at once.

And then she opened her eyes, the emerald green there shocking out here in the middle of all this blue.

"Constantine."

"Tell me," he said, leaning over her, hovering above her lips. "For which of my bad qualities did you first want me?"

"Your outright unfriendliness," she said. "The

scorn with which you looked at me. The hardness. The cruelty of your mouth. The way that it would never smile. Not for me. Oh, how I wanted to taste it. How I wanted to drink in all of your ire for me. I had a man who was sunny and warm, and he would've given me the world. But I wanted the one out of my reach. The one who would not smile."

"Because we are all of us broken," he said. "Wanting what we cannot have. And look at us. Here. Together. What we have is because Alex was broken."

She reached up and touched his face. "No. It's not. I would not have stayed with him. It would've been you. I would've been pregnant either way. And this is where we would be. Don't you think so?"

He growled, pushing the tip of his masculinity into her waiting softness. She gasped, lifting her hips off the deck and he wrapped his arm around her, lifting her toward him as he thrust home, deep and hard. This time knowing that he was the only man to ever be inside of her. This time knowing that she was his, and his alone.

Her rounded belly was between them, a reminder of what had passed through them before.

A reminder of what lay ahead.

But mostly, there was nothing but sensation. But the perfection of being inside of her body.

She moaned, arching up toward him and he leaned down, capturing one nipple into his mouth and sucking hard. A raw gasp escaped her lips, and when he lifted his head, she put her hand on the back of his neck and brought his head down so that he was made to kiss her. And she consumed him. Her tongue searching as their mouths fused, as their desire sparked wildly between them.

She was a wild thing in his arms, and he became a savage.

His thrusts were without tempo or beat. They followed only the roar of his blood.

She gripped his shoulders, her fingernails digging deep as she found her release, as she screamed, a ragged sound in his ear, her internal muscles gripping him tightly, drawing him in deeper. And then, he exploded. On a roar he gave himself up to the desire between them, his jagged breath mingling with hers as he tried to come back to reality. Come back to the present.

He had intended to give her a wedding night. To take her down into the luxurious cabin below and show her what it meant to be his wife.

Perhaps you showed her exactly what it means to be your wife.

Well. Perhaps he had.

And why shouldn't it begin with such

honesty? He had no control where she was concerned.

None at all.

She blinked against the harsh light, and he suddenly felt as if he needed to cover her. Protect her.

He picked her up from the deck, cradling her close to his chest as he carried her down below deck. She barely moved as he spread her over the silken sheets in the well appointed cabin.

It had been his priority that the yacht be luxurious. But he was not the playboy that his brother was. There were many places he entertained women. But not personal places such as this. And certainly not on the island.

She curled partway into a ball, her red hair cascading over her face.

She was his.

There was no question of that now.

And as she drifted off to sleep, and the boat continued on toward the island, he had the feeling that if he could keep her there, separate from the world forever, he might come close to finding happiness.

CHAPTER EIGHT

Morgan had a strange feeling of déjà vu when she opened her eyes and had the distinct sensation that she was in a different place.

This was how it had been when they'd gone to Greece, and again... Wherever they were.

She was lying in bed on Constantine's yacht.

She was sore because he had taken her so roughly on the deck.

Not that it had been unpleasant. It had been... Lovely. Really. He had been...

Everything.

He wanted her. And maybe even wanted the babies.

It had change something for him to know. And not in the way that she had imagined.

She had thought that he would be... Angry. But that wasn't how he was acting. He was acting like a man who had a deep need to possess.

And she was... She wanted to be possessed

by him. That was the thing. It had always been the thing.

He was a twin…

That reality was hovering around the edges of her consciousness and had been ever since he'd said it.

She could look it up. On something. Though, she realized just then that she didn't have her phone. They didn't have anything. She had her wedding dress. And that was all.

But she was naked now.

The door to the cabin opened then, and she scrambled back down to the bed, covering herself with the sheets.

"What are you doing that for?" he asked, his gaze raking over her with hot intent.

"I didn't know who was opening the door."

"There is no one else here. Indeed, there is no one else on the island either."

"The island?"

"Yes. My private island. There is no one else here, and there will not be for the duration, other than when people drop off supplies, and we will have ample warning. It was stocked in preparation for our arrival."

"It was…"

He handed her a lovely, delicately beaded bag. "I believe you will find clothing in there."

He left then, though in the bag she did not really find clothing. Rather she found a lovely if wholly impractical swimsuit, the bottoms resting low below her baby bump, the top barely covering her ample breasts. There was a diaphanous cover that went with it, but it was nearly completely see-through. Still, when she exited the cabin she found it was extremely warm, and if no one else was here…

He was bent over on the deck, wrapping ropes quickly and efficiently into coils. He was wearing a pair of shorts, his shirt discarded. His dark hair looked like he'd been running his fingers through it. Or perhaps like she had been running her fingers through it. And he was… He was gorgeous like this. Out in the wild, not contained in a suit. This was how he looked when he made love. But it was somehow… Illicit and thrilling to see him like this while he was doing something as orderly as working on a yacht.

"You are ready?" He straightened, and her mouth watered as she took in the sight of his broad chest, his flat abs, his bronze skin, covered with just the right amount of hair. She had never really considered herself a fan of chest hair, but Constantine's was a work of art. As indeed was his entire body.

The island itself was glorious. The white sand, palm and cypress trees, along with groves of olives providing shade for the landscape. High up on a hilltop she could just barely see the gleam of glass nestled in the trees.

The house?

Maybe.

"No one is here?"

"No," he said.

"Why?"

He looked at her. "I prize my privacy. I learned that from my grandfather. That a man must protect the space around him, if he is going to work hard, he must hold space."

"Does your father do anything with your family business?"

"No."

He led the way, off the boat, but he did not stop to put on a shirt. Or shoes. He was barefoot, walking up the sandy trail that cut through all those trees, and leading them up toward the house.

He seemed so different here. Relaxed. At home.

"It has all been my responsibility since the death of my grandfather. But he groomed me for this."

"Does it frustrate you?"

His eyes went blank for a moment. "My parents are lovely people. Much in the same way my brother is a lovely person. Was. Gregarious and fun, and not always reliable in the ways that one might like."

"Right," she said softly.

"I learned at a very early age that it was up to me. That I could not count on anyone but myself. Somebody had to take hold of the family fortune. Somebody had to take hold of the family business. It was me. I do not resent that lot in life. There are… There are people who shine brighter, but they do burn out quicker."

She looked at him, at the dark fire that was banked in his eyes. Did he not know that he shone brightly all on his own? He did. He was brilliant.

And yet, she had a feeling if she said that he would reject it. Ignore it. Perhaps even deny it.

"I never had anyone counting on me. Not really. My mother told me that my existence had already failed her. Everything I've ever done has been for me. I don't know what it's like to live for someone else." She put her hand on her stomach. "I wonder if that makes me inherently selfish."

"I see no evidence of your selfishness."

"I don't suppose you've ever seen any evidence of my selflessness either."

He shrugged. "No. But then… You are here."

"You kidnapped me."

"I married you."

"I was going to keep the baby myself. I didn't want you to resent them. Because I know what that's like. That is the most important thing to me, Constantine. That you… That you find it in yourself to love them. Please. Because I know what it's like to be raised by a mother who doesn't love me."

He nodded slowly. "My parents love me very much. And even still, they have done a considerable amount of damage."

"Then I beg you, I beg you to ask yourself what a lack of love might do." She looked at him, beseeching, because she really needed him to understand this. She needed him to know. "Without love, it doesn't mean anything. None of it does. My mother… She was so cold to me. And when I moved out… It was like she was just finished. Done with me. She hasn't spoken to me since. I've gotten in touch with her, and we had a couple of awkward phone calls. But she's never reached out. There's this… Detachment there, and it is brutal. And all I've ever wanted…" Suddenly, tears sprang to her eyes, and she felt ashamed. "All I've ever wanted is for someone to care for me. It is to have people in my life that I cared for. These babies…" And for the first time she felt it. For the first time, she felt her heart swell with love. Felt her chest expand with a deep desire to have these children. With the knowledge that she needed them. That she needed this.

"They will be my chance. My chance to… They're my family. And it is so important to me that you… I do not want you to be like my mother. Not to them. Not to these children. They didn't ask for this, Constantine. They didn't. They didn't ask for me, a girl who's never been loved by anybody. And they didn't ask for…"

"For me?" he asked, working a brow. "No, you're right. They did not ask for a brick wall as a father."

"I didn't mean that. I just mean whatever your baggage, and whatever mine, it is not their fault we carry it."

"You are correct, of course. And I would never want to pass on my particular trauma to anyone, let alone my own children. But that is why I didn't wish to have them."

"I wish that I understood a little bit better. Because we have to do this. Because we're in this together…"

"I told you I was a twin," he said, his voice hard. "Not identical. Fraternal. My sister, Athena… When we were eight years old we were on a beach. My mother was there, and my father. And a nanny, who was chasing Alex around. But not us. My parents were drinking. Partying with friends. It was their favorite sort of vacation, the kind that they were on just before they came to our wedding, in fact. Athena and I were kidnapped. Taken by some of my grandfather's enemies."

She stopped walking. "You what?"

"We were held. For two months."

"Constantine…"

"No one came for us. We waited, and we waited, no one came. There was… We were separated from one another, sometimes. Brought back together when we were terrified and hungry. So that we could see just how much terror was being wrought on the other. And they finally took Athena away from me. And they told me I would never see her again. Not if I didn't pass a test. But I failed. You see, I was left alone in the dark for days. And they told me not to cry, or they would know. But I thought I was alone. And so I cried. Alone by myself, an eight-year-old boy with no hope. With nothing. I cried like a baby. And when my grandfather found us. When he paid the ransom… Athena was nowhere to be found. Yes, whatever happened… My parents' neglect which allow the kidnapping, however long the discussions took place about whether or not they would pay… None of it mattered. Because Athena was gone. And it was because of me."

"You cannot blame yourself. They were evil, vile people."

"It is like your mother," he said. "Your father was a villain, that much is true. But she did not have to punish you. She could have made a different choice. I could have made a different choice. I could've been stronger. But I was weak. I have never been weak, not again. Not since then. I failed her, Morgan. And later I failed Alex. I will never fail my family again. Not ever."

"That's why you said I really wasn't after Alex for his money. Because this was in the news. Wasn't it."

"'Course it was. Athena's death was worldwide news."

"Are you sure she's…"

"She was never seen again. They never found her body, of course. But then… These are the kinds of people that leave no evidence when they wish."

"I'm so sorry. I'm so sorry that you ever felt like that was your fault. That you…"

"It was my fault. That part of it. I'm not afraid."

But he was. Maybe not of taking blame, but of what he might have to do if he didn't. She could see that, clearly. She tried to reconcile the pain he'd been through with the man that was standing in front of her. But of course he'd been through pain. Of course he had. He was not an easy man. And of course he was different than Alex, who would've been so young he wouldn't remember the loss of his sister.

"Alex didn't remember her."

As if he had read her mind. He let out a sharp breath. "It is its own grief. To not remember."

"It must be its own grief to lose a twin. I don't even have a sibling, let alone understand the connection…"

"It is funny," he said. "Because I always imagined that we had a magical bond. So you would think that I would feel as though a limb had been torn from my body because she is gone from this earth. But instead, I still feel the connection there. And I don't know what that means."

"That some bonds are stronger than life and death?"

He shrugged a shoulder.

And just then, the trail rounded the corner, and revealed the front of a massive garden. There were citrus trees and large, broadleaf plants with spots of pink and red. It was magnificent. And behind it, the house, a marvel of design. Glass and large wooden beams. It looked like a part of the landscape, reflecting the ocean down below. Nearly hidden, constructed as it was.

"This is mine. Every other place you've been... It was the family's. But this is mine."

And she had the sense that she now knew him better than just about anyone else on earth.

Athena would've known him.

Her heart ached for him. For that loneliness and being the one left behind. What a horrible thing. A horrible fate. A horrible tragedy. And she had thought that he was a mountain who felt nothing. That maybe the truth was he was a man who had felt far too much pain. Far too much loss, after so much love. And he had closed himself down because it was more than he could bear. Because it was more than anyone could ever be expected to bear.

"Let's go."

They walked through the garden, and up the front steps and the doors parted as he approached.

"Facial recognition," he said.

Her mouth dropped in awe as they stepped inside to the tropical oasis. The floors were made of stone, plants climbing up the walls inside, over beams that ran across the ceiling. There was warm wood, a sharp contrast to all the glass around them, the pristine beauty outside.

It was quiet. They really were the only ones here.

"This is not at all what I expected."

"What did you expect?"

"More marble, I suppose."

"Marble is what my parents like. I... Especially here, I wanted it to be about our surroundings."

"If you could live anywhere it would be here, wouldn't it?"

"When I was kidnapped, being kept alone was terrifying. In the end, I learned something from it. That sometimes solitude is the only way to find peace, and if a man can learn to be alone with himself, then he can do anything. I learned to find purpose in solitude."

And to never cry, she imagined. To never let himself feel anything unfettered. To conquer the deepest fear that he held because he could not ever let himself be controlled by it. Not again.

He didn't have to say that. But she knew all the same. She just did.

"You spend a lot of time alone," she said.

He grinned. "It is how I like it."

No. It was how it had to be. That was another thing she could clearly see. Why deny himself simply because he was paying a penance? She grabbed his hand, put it on her stomach. "They're yours."

He nodded slowly. "I know. I do not doubt."

"Why don't you doubt me now, Constantine,

when you did before? I could easily be lying to you about the fact that I was a virgin."

His expression turned fierce. "You are not, though."

"No," she said softly. "I'm not."

"My desire for you is beyond measure," he said. "This is my sanctuary, and I do not bring anyone here. But I wished to bring you. Just like myself on your beautiful body. And to... Keep you from the world."

And why wouldn't he? The world had been so unbearably cruel to him.

"Aren't you angry," she asked. "With your parents. For allowing you to be kidnapped?"

His eyes went blank. "It does no good. And they are all the family I have."

"Not anymore," she said softly.

They weren't alone. He knew her secrets, and she knew his. They weren't alone.

"I must go. I have some work to see to."

"Work?"

"I have an office upstairs. There is Internet here."

"Oh. Of course. I will..."

"There is food prepared in the fridge. You are welcome to it. It should be prepared and ready for you. You may also swim in any one of the pools, and explore the gardens. You will find many fresh fruits there that you may help yourself to. You may also take a nap. There is a room prepared for you."

"Thank you. It means something to me, that you always have a place for me."

His face went hard. "I take care of what's mine."

And then he went upstairs, his footsteps echoing against the wood as he went. And left alone, she could hear the sound of the waves beyond the windows, and nothing more.

This was the kind of isolation Constantine preferred. And she understood why.

And she had to wonder if he had to carry so much anger at himself because...

Because of the family he had left. *We will be his family now.*

She held that truth close, wishing that she could make it his truth as well.

CHAPTER NINE

"WHAT THE HELL HAPPENED?"

"It's complicated."

"Hell, boy," his father said. "I have time for complicated."

Funny, because he rarely seemed to have time for anything but indulgence, but now that there was a hint of a scandal, he had time. He banished that thought. He was simply raw because he had been talking about Athena. Because it was so clear that Morgan had not understood why he had to bear the burden of his own culpability in the situation. Why it was important.

"It will not make you happy," he said, and something dark and gleeful rose up inside of him.

Aren't you angry at them...?

"Don't tell me the babies are not Alex's," his father said.

"No," Constantine said. "They are not."

"Dammit. I don't know what we'll tell your mother. She's going to be heartbroken…"

"Oh," Constantine said. "They're still your grandchildren."

A pause settled between them.

"What are you saying?"

"They're mine."

"Yours?"

"Twins, father. And mine."

"How is that possible?"

"The usual way these things are possible. Your golden boy betrayed her. She went to his room, and he was already with another woman. And so she came to my room."

"And you could not leave your brother's girlfriend alone? She was the love of his life, Constantine."

"So much so that he was with another woman the night he died," Constantine said. "I know you love Alex, I do too. But that does not make him perfect, and it certainly does not absolve him of his betrayal of Morgan."

"Did you not betray him? You could've waited for the dust to settle."

"But I didn't. I wanted her. And I had her. I had still imagined that they were Alex's children. But they are not."

"This…"

"You can say it. You were disappointed because you prefer Alex to me."

"And I am disappointed because your brother will never get another chance to have children. You could've had children with anyone."

"And Alex could've chosen to fuck his girlfriend and not someone else. And had he not been with someone else, he would still be alive."

Barely leashed rage rose up inside of him.

"It is perhaps best if your mother does not know."

"You would have me deny my own children to my mother to preserve the fantasy you have."

There was a long uncomfortable silence on the other end of the phone. His father was not a cool man, but he was confronting him head-on, and he knew his father did not care for such things.

"Well?"

"I will think about it."

"I may not give you the choice."

"Alex…"

"You think about things for too long," Constantine said. "You are inactive for too long."

"I was not there," his father said, his voice suddenly turning to ice. "You were the one that was there. You were the one that failed the test."

His father had never been cruel to him before, but this was certainly edging close to it. Of course...he had fired the first shot.

"I've accepted my part in it," Constantine said. "I do not deny my own weakness. But that is not a skill I learned from you."

His father made a wrenching sound that chilled Constantine's soul. "I know it. Don't you think I don't know my own weakness, Constantine? To have lost two children as I have... I thought... I did believe that we would have this part of your brother."

"Sadly," Constantine said. "It is only me."

"Your mother..."

"Leave it for now," he said.

He hung up the phone and went to the window, looking out at the sea below. He had known they would not take this well. He was not taking it well.

For this very reason.

There was a strange, cloying fear that threatened to choke him. Something in the way that he breathed and moved.

These children were to be his responsibility. And then there was Morgan. Morgan who...

None of this was her fault. He had been angry with her. For appealing to him. Angry with her for daring to be beautiful when she belonged to his brother. When the fact of the matter was, she had been his downfall from the very beginning, simply by breathing. And it was more than her belonging to his brother, it was…

But now she's yours. She is yours, and you can keep her separate from the world.

Perhaps… Perhaps his father was right. Perhaps allowing the world to believe that these were his brother's children…

Maybe it would be better. Maybe it would keep them safe.

Because one thing Constantine knew for sure.

That which he loved ended up lost.

He could not bear for that fate to meet his children.

Morgan hadn't seen Constantine all day. She had found a fruit tray in the fridge, and she had spent the day grazing on it, and she would have said that she couldn't be satisfied by something so alarmingly healthy, not in this state where she craved carbs and cheese, but here on the island it felt somehow glamorous, and she found she enjoyed it.

She didn't bother to change out of the bikini that he had given her, because why? There was no one here.

She was beginning to feel like he wasn't here either. She missed him.

She had told him, and his response had been… So not what she had expected. He seemed angry with her, but desirous at the same time, and her own feelings had been thrown into a wild wind and whipped around until she couldn't sort them out.

And the longer she sat by herself the more she wondered if she... She did not want to. But the more she sat by herself the more she wondered if she needed to contact her own mother.

She was becoming a mother.

And it made her ache to reach out to the woman who had given birth to her. The woman who had not nurtured her.

The woman who had left her feeling scarred and tragic, but who had also... Given life to her. It was so complicated, and there was part of her that wanted to understand the complication as deeply as she could.

She didn't have her phone.

Everything had been left at the wedding. And she knew that meant seeking out Constantine.

She walked up the stairs, wood planks that seemed to float in midair, held there by taut wire, and stood on the landing for a long while, looking out the vast windows at the jewel bright sea below.

She did not know how she had come to be in this place. A waitress who had wanted little more than to survive, a woman who had been so desperate not to repeat the mistakes of her mother. But she had. It was only because the man was wealthy and insisted on claiming his children. That was the difference.

It made her feel... Shamed.

Because she wasn't better than her mother, she had made an easier mistake, fallen into a happier accident.

She had been ruled entirely by her desires the night that she was with Constantine for the first time. And she hadn't behaved much better since. She had not resisted him at all when he had taken her down on the yacht deck. She had resisted him at no point. She had seen him, and she had wanted him. She had thought nothing for the future.

She heard the door open, and as they were the only two people on the whole of the island, she knew it was him. She went toward the sound, down a long corridor that stretched over the first floor, a suspension bridge that lent itself to the open-air feeling of the house.

And then it was closed off, a few doors leading to other rooms undoubtedly. And around the corner, she met Constantine. It was strange, to be in this enclosed place where there were so many other open spaces. And seeing him like this... She could barely breathe.

He was not wearing a suit, but he had put a shirt on. A white one, only buttoned up partway.

She took a visual tour of his masculine beauty. All of that skin and black chest hair.

He was truly a stunning specimen of a man. And oh, how she wanted him. Even now, grappling with these hard truths.

The whims of fate. Accidents.

Her own lack of superiority.

"I need to call my mother," she said.

"I see."

"All of my things are back on the mainland. I don't have my phone."

"Do you know her number?"

She did. Only because her mother had had the same number since Morgan was a child.

"Yes."

"You may use my phone."

"Okay. Thank you."

"I spoke to my father."

She winced. "And?"

"He is not happy with me. That much is certain."

"I'm certain he is unhappy with me too."

His face took on a strange, serious cast. "No. His dissatisfaction lies wholly with me. Trust me."

She blinked, feeling emotion pooling at the corners of her eyes. "I am complicit in what happened between us. If they are angry at you…"

"He thinks it would be best if my mother

didn't know the truth. And I have thought about it, and I think that is perhaps for the best."

"Constantine… How can we possibly keep this to ourselves?"

"I wonder if… I do wonder if the children would be safer if they are not believed to be mine."

"Safer… Who do you think might come for them?"

"The same people who came for me when I was a child."

"But surely…"

"They are a powerful crime family. And the vendetta that they had against my grandfather was very real. I now occupy that position."

"Do you really think concealing the fact that you're their father will help?"

"I don't know. I have no way of knowing that. All I know is… My sister…"

"I understand," she said, even though she didn't. Not quite. Except he was afraid, this man. This rock. For the children that she carried, and perhaps, she simply needed to acknowledge that. Listen to it. But it hurt her. To think that he might not acknowledge them. Because that did skim far too close to her own truth. To her own life.

A father who never wanted anything to do with her…

But no. He would be there for them. He would.

"You are using this to distance yourself," she said.

He looked at her, his expression sharp. "What do you mean?"

"You never wanted children, Constantine, and I do think I understand why. I understand that you've been through things that… That would break lesser men. And you are not broken. But what I do wonder is this… What I do wonder is if this is an opportunity for you to pull away from being a father. And you are their father."

"I know that," he said, his voice hard.

"I didn't want to be a mother," she said. "I didn't. That relationship for me is… It is difficult, and it is complicated. And it hurts me. And I don't know if I will be a better mother to my children. Or maybe I will be, by default, because I don't have to worry about money. Because I don't have to worry about how we live. Maybe that's the only reason I'll be better. And does that really make me better?"

"I don't understand. Why would it matter. Better is better."

"Is it? I have spent so many years being angry at my own mother, and when I found out I was pregnant I could not muster one kernel of joy. Not in the deepest part of myself. I was so sad. Because I knew that I had done the exact same thing. Gotten pregnant by accident by a man who wanted nothing to do with his own child. Children. It never occurred to me of course that I might be pregnant with two. And if I had been left on my own to care for them, would I have sunk into bitterness just like her? Trying to care for two children on my own, trying to balance the demands of caring for them and having a job? And what would have kept me from that same bitterness?"

"I will," he said.

"Your money will?"

"Does it matter? Is it not all the same?"

He handed her his phone. "Call her."

And the thing that saddened and worried her the most was the fact that she really did think money might be the difference, and it felt so… It made her mouth taste like ash.

"Is there a place that I can go…"

"Your bedroom is just here."

He walked back around the corner and pushed open the door to a phenomenal glass room that stuck out high over the hillside, with trees all around it and the ocean at the front.

"Oh…"

"Every room in this home is designed to be part of nature."

"It's beautiful. Everything around me is beautiful all the time when I'm with you."

And she knew she sounded sad, because she was a little bit sad.

He regarded her for a long moment, and then closed the door behind her.

With trembling fingers, she called her mother. The phone rang three times, and she was not sure if she was hoping her mother would answer or… Or not.

But she did.

"Hello?"

"Hi, Mom," Morgan said.

"Morgan?" Her mother was questioning it, not because she had other children, but because Morgan hadn't spoken to her in a couple of years.

"Yeah. I just… I needed to tell you some things."

"Oh?"

It didn't surprise her that her mother hadn't seen the news. Why would she? She didn't follow the lifestyles of the rich and famous. It only upset her.

"I got married."

"Well," her mom said. "Good for you. Though, I would've thought you'd invite me to the wedding."

"It all happened really quickly. I'm… I'm pregnant."

"Oh," her mom said, and there was a wealth

of hurt in that one sound. Maybe because the father of Morgan's children had married her.

"Twins," Morgan said.

"Twins don't run in the family," she said.

"They run in his," she said. "I'm due in four months. But they'll probably be early. I guess twins are like that."

"So it didn't happen all that quickly, then?" her mom said.

"Well. I guess not."

"Did you just want to share the news?"

"I wanted… I wanted to ask you something, but I don't know how to ask. I'm worried I…"

"What?"

"Did you love me ever? Or did I only ever just make your life hard? And was it the money? Was it that he didn't support you? What was it?"

"Of course I love you," her mom said. "I wouldn't have worked so hard to take care of you if I didn't."

Guilt overcame Morgan then, because she had always been so bitter about how hard her mother had made it seem, and that had made Morgan feel like a burden. But… She supposed that was true. Her mom hadn't had to take care of her. She had made a choice, and that choice had been to raise her.

And she made mistakes that had left Morgan feeling raw and wounded. And she was looking for something... Something magical in her own self that would make her know she wouldn't do the same thing to her own children. But right now she just felt... Well, she felt guilty. That she had judged her mother so harshly. That she had been so certain in her own superiority, and all of that was breaking down slowly as she faced the reality of her own situation, of her own limitations. But even more now that she was on the phone with her mother asking her directly if she loved her.

"It's just that you never seemed very happy to have me," Morgan said.

The words tripped clumsily off her tongue.

"I don't know that I've ever been very happy," her mom responded.

The words lanced Morgan. "Why?"

Her mother drew a tight breath in. "I've never thought about it. Not really."

"What do you live for?"

"I get up every day. I go to work. We had our apartment, and it was never much, but we had something. I felt like I did something by keeping you safe. And making sure you had food to eat. But I suppose I've always felt lonely. At least a bit."

"I'm sorry," Morgan said. "I'm sorry if I've been part of you being lonely. I guess I should've been there for you. But I didn't know if you wanted me to be."

"I've never liked asking for it," her mom said. "I begged your father to love me. And I've never felt so small in my life than when he refused. To ask for someone to care and to have them tell you they won't…"

"Did you love my father?"

"Yes. Because I was a fool. And I let that decide how I felt every day for far too long. And by the time I decided not to, keeping things closed down inside myself was a habit. I never wanted to ask for more. Not again."

"I want you to be involved with the kids," Morgan said. And that wasn't why she'd called. But she realized that it needed to be why. Because she was lonely too, and she still had her mother. Her mother wasn't evil, she was just… Sad. And now that Morgan had dispensed with any idea that she was superior, she couldn't look at her the same way. She was just human. Frail and fallible like Morgan was.

And Morgan didn't want anger or sadness to dictate the way she was with her own children. And she shouldn't let it dictate the way she was with her mother, either.

"Well I would like that."

"I'll have to tell you the whole story. Sometime. I'm in Greece, though. Well, I think I'm in Greece."

"Greece?"

"He's... He's from a very old family here. Actually, I'm on an island right now."

"An island?"

"Yes. And..." A big needy feeling opened up inside of her. One that she had always despised. "I do love you," she said to her mom.

"I love you too," she said. "I always have. It was hard. Raising you. But I did the best I could."

She believed it. She believed it then, because it felt right to believe it. She believed it then because what was the benefit of disbelieving? She believed it then because that was how she was going to look at it.

Because she wanted to begin to heal, and she thought this was the best way to do it.

Hanging on certainly wasn't going to do it. Being caught up in her own hurt wasn't going to do it. It was just going to keep that hurt fresh. It was just going to keep her right where she was, and she couldn't afford that. She had to move on. She had to. For the sake of her children. For the sake of herself.

"We'll... We'll talk more often," Morgan said.

"Okay," her mom responded.

"And I'll let you know when I get close to… When the babies are coming."

"Thank you."

They hung up the phone, and Morgan looked out at the water, and thought again about how far she'd come. But right then, she felt like she still had astronomically far to go. So many complicated things to sort out.

Constantine didn't want to claim the children as his, and she had talked to her mother about things she had never thought she would.

Her mother had been… Lonely for her father for so many years, and she had been protecting herself. And that gave Morgan pause.

What would it be like to live with Constantine but not have his emotions? Would it begin to wear on her? Would holding herself back and trying to make herself not care affect the way she was with her children? She didn't want to do that with her mom, not anymore. Didn't want to hold back because she was hurt, because she had the feeling that that had been part of compounding their loneliness. She didn't blame herself. There were two people involved in the relationship, after all. She moved over to the closet in the room and opened it. And inside there was a bright blue dress, designed to flow and skim over the wearer's body.

And it made her want to be the woman that

could wear it. That would look beautiful in it. That would tempt a man in it. That was the problem. In the middle of all these questions about motherhood, there was just this whole thing with him, and she wished they could've worked it out without... Marriage and children being in the mix. God knew it would've been easier.

Maybe that was what she needed to do. Maybe she needed to set aside the conversation with her mother. Maybe they needed to set aside the fact that they had married one another, the fact that they were having children, the fact that... All of the facts, actually. Maybe they needed to put it all away and simply be here. On an island. Two people alone. Perhaps the only people in the world. And see what happened.

And she proposed that she would do just that.

CHAPTER TEN

IT WAS TORTUROUS, working while here on the island. He didn't often do it. But it was the perfect vehicle by which to avoid Morgan, which was what he was doing at the moment.

Coward.

Perhaps.

But he had just told her that he might not claim the children.

Guilt ate at him. Because he wondered if she was right, and he rarely wondered if anyone but himself was right. If perhaps he had never considered himself a coward.

Not in the years since his kidnapping.

He had been weak then, and he had gone out of his way to never be in the years since.

He laughed at himself now.

He made his way down the stairs, and he smelled something phenomenal.

But what he saw when he made his way down to the landing was more exciting than the prospect of dinner. It was Morgan, standing by a set table that was surrounded by lush gardens, partly concealed. She was wearing a blue dress that hugged her curves, her red hair flowing freely. Her pale shoulders were exposed, and he felt a strong urge to count the freckles on them. To memorize her body. To make her his.

"What is all this?" he asked as he stepped outside.

"I thought that I would… Make us dinner. It's been a long couple of days. And we're here. On a private island. And there's nothing… There's nothing but you and me, Constantine. We called our parents. We did our duty. We…had the wedding. And now we're here. I am not your brother's girlfriend. And you are not my boyfriend's disapproving older brother. You are Constantine, and I'm Morgan. And maybe we need a moment to figure out what that means."

And he wanted that, he realized. Wanted to take that moment where it was only the two of them and exist in it. Put down the trauma from the past and let the memories recede into nothing. What if she was just a woman, a beautiful woman that he wanted. Standing there. Everything he'd ever desired. And he never gave in to temptation. It wasn't who he was.

But right then, he did.

He let her words paint a picture of a fantasy that he knew couldn't exist, and never would.

"You cooked?"

"There was some lovely steak, and beautiful vegetables, and I've had to cook for myself for a long time. I know my way around the kitchen, though I have to say yours is glorious."

"I do not cook," he said. "I didn't realize the kitchen was particularly glorious."

"What is the point of it," she asked, a funny little smile on her face. "Having so many glorious things when you don't even know how glorious they are?"

In spite of himself, he felt his mouth kick upward into a smile. He crossed the space where she was and held her chair out for her. "Why don't you have a seat."

"All right."

The sky was low in the sky, and the pink light of it setting over the water suffused the air around them. Warm and close and intoxicating. The scent of flowers hung in the air, or maybe it was just her.

And he felt like he was under her spell for a moment. And he was not a man who had ever believed in such things.

She was right. He was surrounded by fantasy at all times. His mother's ridiculous fairy room, and all of the opulence they indulged themselves in. And yet he didn't… He didn't allow himself those moments. He did not allow himself fantasy.

So perhaps for just this moment.

Perhaps. All of his seriousness had not protected Alex, after all.

He had thought that it would. He had changed after the loss of Athena, and he had been certain he could keep harm from ever befalling his family again. But he hadn't managed it. Not with all of his determination and all of his strength, so what then did he think the result would be now?

The world was cruel.

And because of that cruelty he had not even allowed himself a moment to look at the beauty. Until her. He had looked at her and he had been unable to stop.

"I've never seen opulence as a gift," he said. "It was simply a fact of my existence. And I saw the hard things in the world early. And opulence did not save me from them."

"I understand that," she said. "I really do. But believe me when I tell you, the lack of it was something I always felt. In part because my mother was so keenly aware of it."

"I have been surrounded my entire life by opulence and remarkable beauty. And so private islands and stunning vistas, ornately themed rooms, and beautiful homes… They do not signify. But you… The moment that I saw you, Morgan, I felt like I was seeing something truly original. Truly new, and it was better than any gilded statue could ever be. And having you… What is forbidden to me? I'm a man with money and power. Nothing is forbidden to me. But you were. That is a novelty that far outstrips any well-appointed kitchen."

"Are you saying I'm your one indulgence?"

"You have been that, yes. And I… I have reveled in you, that much is certain."

"I don't think I've ever been anyone's indulgence," she said, her eyes looking glassy, and he did not know why such a… Such a basic compliment, borderline crude would produce that result.

"I'm sure many men would've liked you to be."

"But I didn't want to be theirs. I suppose. And it doesn't mean anything if you don't also want it. When I met you…"

"Why don't we pretend that you only just did?" Because he liked fantasy. Even if it was ridiculous.

"Okay. Then let's pretend I don't know anything about you. What was your favorite ice cream when you were a child?"

He laughed. He couldn't help himself. He was caught entirely off guard by the mischievous gleam in her eyes, by the little smile on her face, and by the mention of ice cream, of all things.

"I don't know," he said.

"That's ridiculous. Of course you know. Everyone had a favorite ice cream. What was it you ordered or asked for at the grocery store or...do billionaire children go to the grocery store?"

"No," he said, memories beginning to crowd his mind.

He realized he didn't know because he didn't allow himself to think about his childhood. Because in the before, there was Athena, and thinking of her was like a dagger in his soul. And in the after, he had no longer been a child. Not really.

But he could remember, he could remember his grandfather taking himself and Athena and little Alex to get an ice cream cone at a shop on the beach. The same beach that they had been taken from later. But he didn't focus on what had come after. And he didn't think about what had come before. He thought only of that moment. And the joy that he had felt in it. And he remembered the ice cream.

"Chocolate. With caramel. That's what I would get at this little place on the beach. And my grandfather would let us each get a cone. And I cannot think of ice cream without also thinking of the beach. Of sand, and of the sun melting it so quickly that we had to eat impossibly fast. Yes. That's what I think of." He could see the ice cream in his mind, rolling down the cone, down his hand, onto the gritty sand below.

"My mother would get me some sometimes when we went to the grocery store," she said. "It was only a quarter, and I never got a cone, because if you got a cup you got much more. They would overfill it. Praline pecan. That was my favorite. Also caramel, but with vanilla ice cream. And those candy nuts. That is a memory from my childhood where I felt truly happy."

"And me as well."

"Very different memories, but that makes us seem more the same than different, doesn't it?"

He nodded slowly. "Yes. It does."

"Favorite cartoon."

"Cartoons?"

"Yes."

"I don't... I do not think I watched cartoons."

"I am certain that you did," she said. "I personally love this entire block of cartoons on the public access channel. And actually, I suppose the one that I loved wasn't actually a cartoon. It was about a dog. And it was light action. He dressed up in costumes for every book that he went into. I loved that. I wanted my imagination to be that real. I think that's what captured me about the different things that I loved."

"I suppose my imagination did not have to be so strong," he said.

Though as he said that he had the impression of being in a playroom, early in the morning, snuggled up in blankets, with Athena next to him. "There was a cartoon about ponies. And they had magic powers. My sister liked to watch that. And I would sit with her. I did not enjoy it, of course."

"Of course not," Morgan said.

"I preferred cartoons that had some sword fighting."

"Naturally."

"We had quite the home theater. And we used to screen films down there. My parents were always like children with things like that. So excited to show us the latest big cartoon that could otherwise only be seen in theaters."

"Well, that is far beyond anything I could've imagined."

"There was one about a woman who dressed as a man to save her country. That had a lot of sword fighting and I liked it. It reminded me... You remind me of that."

"I have not dressed up as a man," Morgan said.

"Perhaps not. But you are willing to fight. No matter what. Every step of the way."

"I think that is one of the nicest compliments anyone has ever given me. Though sometimes I'm tired of fighting."

Me too.

But the word stuck in his throat. He didn't have the luxury of being tired of fighting. He didn't know why he felt that. What was he even fighting for? To atone for the dark and gritty things in the past that he could not make right, no matter how hard he tried.

To do what his grandfather had told him. When there had been no more ice cream and no more Athena. When he'd looked at him with fierce eyes and told him he had to be a man now. Hard. He had to have control. He had to handle things.

It was up to him to make things right.

To live right.

To be the Kamaras man that his grandfather needed him to be.

He just knew that it always felt like a fight. One that he seemed to continually lose. And he was not a man who was given to such things.

He had been a success taking over his family's business. He had been a success in managing his parents' spending and excesses, and Alex's too. But in the end he had not been able to keep Alex safe. So what did it all mean? And what did it all matter?

It was strange how not talking about it, housesitting with Morgan and trying to interact as strangers, brought up things that he tried not to think about any other time.

"We don't have to fight now," she said.

She smiled at him, and he realized they hadn't been eating. They had only been talking.

The dinner that she had made him was truly wonderful. "I don't know that anyone's ever made dinner for me before."

"That's ridiculous. Don't you have chefs? People make dinner for you all the time."

"That's different," he said. "They are paid to cook for the family, or for me I suppose in the abstract sense. You just decided to cook for me."

She ducked her head, and color mounted in her cheeks, and he felt an answering desire rise inside of him. He did not have a name for what it was he wanted. He was reminded yet again of being a child. On that same day he'd gone and gotten the ice cream. And they had gone into an aquarium, and he stood on the other side of the glass staring at the colorful, teeming world of fish. And he had felt like he wanted to step through that glass, for beyond that was a true mystery. Something truly off-limits, something that he could not just be given. And that was how he felt now. As a little boy staring at something brilliant and wild and intangible and knowing that a thick sheet of glass separated him from it, and that even if it were not there, it was not something that he could possess. Not something that he could experience.

She was right there, and yet it felt like she was in another world. Felt like she was apart from him.

He wanted to rage, because he did not like things that were out of his control. He did not like things he could not understand.

And there was something about Morgan that he could not understand. Something about her that he could not touch.

"I wanted to cook for you," she said. "I wanted to give you something."

"Why? What have I ever given you?"

"You're giving me children." She smiled ruefully. "Sorry. I suppose I'm not doing a very good job of acting like we just met."

"I don't care. Enough games. Why would you do this for me? Why do you... Why do you care at all?"

"I don't know how not to, Constantine. If I did that I never would've slept with you."

"You were angry with Alex."

"I wanted you. I told you that already. Yes, I was angry with Alex, but I was a virgin, do you honestly think I would only sleep with you to get back at your brother? I did it because I wanted something that was mine. For me. I did it because I wanted to indulge myself after a lifetime of total control. And you were the gift that I wanted. You were… The ice cream. Just there to be an indulgence. So I suppose we're the same on that score. That you were my indulgence too."

"Morgan…"

"And now we are having these children. And nothing about the way we've begun is normal, or makes sense, or is a way that people should carry on. But I don't know how to go back and be like everyone else. And maybe we won't. Maybe we can't be. Maybe a billionaire who ends up with a waitress can never be…" She shook her head. "I'm sorry. Maybe those are the wrong words."

"What words?"

"Ends up with. I feel like that implies romance and happy endings. And that isn't necessarily us."

"What you are is mine," he said. "There will be no question of there being other people in this union, you understand that, don't you?"

"I don't want anyone else. I never have. You were the only man that I have ever wanted."

"You were ready to sleep with Alex."

"I liked him and I thought it was time. But I didn't think at all when it came to you. It was about desire, and I was completely over-whelmed by it."

But that wasn't it. It wasn't the answer. It wasn't what he felt when he looked at her. That unsatisfied sensation that made him feel rocked to his core.

It wasn't just desire, because... Even if he had never experienced desire like this before, he knew what it was to want a woman.

Do you? Can you even remember what it's like to want anyone other than Morgan?

No. He couldn't. From the moment he had seen her he'd been consumed with her. He had not touched another woman since the first time he had seen Morgan almost a year ago.

The realization stunned him.

"I have not been with anyone else since the moment we met," he said, and he had not in-tended to say that to her, had not meant to say it out loud, but for some reason honesty had felt... It had felt necessary then. Perhaps because he was sitting there grappling with the truth of it in himself.

"You... You haven't been?"

"No. I haven't wanted anyone. Not since the moment my brother first brought you home. I thought it was quite a cruelty. That a woman on his arm should capture my attention so. But you must understand, I never expected to see you again after that first time. And still, you haunted me. You haunted my dreams. In a rather effortless fashion."

"And you wanted to have a marriage in name only?"

"I did not see what the alternative could possibly be."

"You didn't want me to be carrying his children."

"It doesn't matter. It would've been better. It would be right."

"You didn't want me to be carrying his children because you want them."

"I should not."

"Who cares about should and shouldn't, Constantine? We have never followed that guideline. It has never mattered to us. No matter that we might have wanted it to, it never has."

He could not deny the truth of what she was saying, even if it gouged at him. Of course he wanted the children to be his, the same as he wanted her to be his, but it didn't matter. Except it did. All of it mattered. No matter how he told himself it should not and could not. It did.

She was pregnant with his babies.

And he wanted to believe that redemption was what was on the other side of that glass. But did it matter if it was? He had her. She was here. They were his children, they were not Alex's.

And just perhaps he did not owe his brother a legacy. Perhaps Alex should've guarded his own legacy. Perhaps his brother should have managed things, taken care of himself. Well, perhaps that. The children were his, and she was his. And she had wanted him above Alex. And suddenly, the beast inside of him roared.

He wanted her. In his bed. Tonight. Now.

"I hope there is no dessert," he said.

"Why not?"

"Because I do not have the patience to eat it."

He reached across the table then, drew her to him, and kissed her on the mouth.

She made a muffled cry as he did so, and then she stood, rounding the table quickly and scrabbling into his lap. He kissed her like he was dying. Like she was water and he was a man dying of thirst out in the middle of the desert.

He kissed her because there was nothing else he could do. He kissed her, because he wanted nothing else.

And she was like a flame in his arms, hot and perfect, and when he pressed his mouth to hers he whispered, "Mine."

He picked her up and carried her into the house, up the stairs, and he took her straight to his room. His room. Because he had been a fool to believe that he would ever keep her in her own room.

No. She was his.

And this was beyond the desire that he had felt for her on the deck. When he had claimed her on the yacht fresh with the knowledge in his mind that she had never been with another man.

He had been consumed then by the primal urge to claim her, but it had still not been this. This wholehearted acceptance of the fact that she was his.

That there was no part of her that belonged to Alex, least of all their children.

And that he was… And that he was glad of it. That he would want it no other way.

He laid her down on the white sheets, her dress like spilled ink across the pristine fabric. Her red hair as a flame.

She was exquisite. And he had never known such need.

"Please," she whispered.

Begging for him.

Morgan was begging for him.

And he felt…

She had made him dinner. And she begged for him.

He had no shortage of women in his life, in his bed. Women who came to him because they wanted a powerful man. And he was not foolish enough to be unaware of the fact that physically he was the sort of man women desired. It was simply the way he was put together, and he never had vanity about it, nor humility.

It was simply part of who he was, the same as the money, the same as the power. But that Morgan wanted him suddenly mattered.

That it was her begging for his touch, that mattered.

And why? She had said it herself. She was a waitress. He was a billionaire.

And yet, he felt in the moment that the power was with her. He stripped his clothes off, and came down to lie beside her, running his hands over her curves. Then slowly, ever so slowly, he pulled the strap on her dress down, displaying one pale breast for his enjoyment. And then the other.

He ran his hands slowly over them, flicking his thumbs over her nipples. Watching as she gasped with need. She arced up off the bed, a live wire of desire, and he pulled the dress down more, revealing the rounded curve of her stomach. And truly, in that moment it struck him, that she was carrying his children. His children. His blood. His blood in the way that Athena had been. And they were twins. A boy and a girl. He put his hands on her body then, watched as they covered the baby bump.

"I will protect you," he said.

And he kissed her there then, resting his forehead right there. "I swear upon my life. I will not let anything happen to you."

A vow. Both to Morgan, and to his children.

"You cannot take that all on yourself," she whispered. She ran her hand over his hair, down his jaw, and tilted his face up to look at her.

"Yes, I can," he said.

"You don't control everything," she said.

He growled, making his way over her body, grabbing her wrists and capturing them in one hand, trapping them up over her head, her breasts rising up toward him as he did so.

"I will protect you. Because you are mine. My wife. The mother of my children."

"And will you tell the world?"

"Yes," he said, his voice a growl. "Because I will not have anyone thinking that you were ever anyone's but mine."

"Constantine."

She said his name. His name. And on her lips it was like magic. And it ignited a piece of his soul, made him feel alive in a way he never had before.

He was overcome. By the desperate certainty that he would create a new heaven and a new earth all in the name of keeping her safe. Of keeping her with him.

He was powerful, and he had always taken it for granted. She made it feel essential. Because he would use that power, he would use any means necessary to bind her to him.

And he knew that beyond a shadow of a doubt.

He continued to trap her hands as he leaned in and kissed her mouth, pouring all of that intensity into her. He didn't have the words for it. *Nothing but mine.* That word echoed inside of him, over and over. Mine. He kissed her neck, her collarbone, down to the soft swell of her breasts, and he sucked her there until she moaned with desire.

He tormented her with his mouth, tormented them both. She was everything. Perfection. The most glorious, delectable treat he had ever tasted. And he was enthralled. He had to have her. He had to.

He thrust inside her then, the tight, wet heat of her body testing his control.

"Mine," he said. "Mine."

He claimed her like that, over and over again. Until they were both mindless. And just as her pleasure reached the boiling point, his own unraveled, and they both went over the edge together.

CHAPTER ELEVEN

MORGAN WAS SORE and sated the next day, her whole body replete from making love with Constantine all night.

She had stayed in his bed. It was the first time they had gone to sleep together. But when she woke up, he wasn't there. And she felt bereft. Wondering if the connection that she felt with him last night had just been something she'd imagined. She kept coming back to that thought she'd had earlier. That what she wanted was for him to have feelings for her. She was sitting with that, while considering all that it meant for her. Especially when taking into account the revelations that she'd gotten from her mother. It should have—almost—made her more afraid of her feelings. But that wasn't the effect. She was afraid of being hurt.

She didn't know if she could reach him. She just wasn't certain.

But she wanted… She wanted.

And last night had been... Well, she had loved their conversation. He had seemed younger. More human. And then a switch had flipped inside of him and he had gone all intense. But of course, he hadn't talked about that.

She got out of bed and realized she didn't have any clothes in here. And because there was no one else here... There was no reason to be concerned. She walked out of the bedroom, stark naked, and began to head toward her room. But there, of course, was Constantine, standing at the end of the hall, looking at her with dark, fathomless eyes.

"You're awake."

"Yes," she said, heat rising up in her body.

"I like you this way. If you aren't cold, perhaps this is how you should be for me all day."

"Possessive," she said.

Mine.

He had said that, repeatedly. Over and over again.

"Yes," he said.

"Why?"

"Because you're carrying my children, *agape*."

She knew enough to know that meant *love* in Greek.

But she was not his love.

No, what had passed between them last night

had been something dark and intense, and nothing half so sweet. There had been a moment. When they had spoken of ice cream, and she had...

He was fathomless, this man who was her husband.

He had told her about his sister, about his deep pain. But she didn't feel closer to knowing him because of that. It was when he had stopped and spoken of things he'd enjoyed that she had found something she recognized. It was only then.

"I'm not certain you would get anything done," she said.

"What do I need to get done?"

She laughed at that. "I don't know. You were awfully busy yesterday."

"And now I'm not busy today."

And he wasn't. They spent the day at the beach, and after she got over her initial shyness, and her concern over being sunburned—which he dealt with by rubbing lotion all over her body—she enjoyed being bare underneath the sun. He joined her, only he looked like he was part of the landscape. Like he belonged. He looked as if he had been born there. Poseidon, maybe. A god of the sea...cut and bronzed and glorious.

And it was perfect like this. They spoke little,

feeding each other fruit and making love in the sand. Swimming in the waves.

But the problem with that was it gave her a chance to interrogate her heart.

She loved him. And love, she realized then was the seed of joy.

That joy that had taken root in her spirit and begun to drive out the bitterness she'd been so afraid of.

She had been on the verge of admitting that to herself quite some time ago. But it was more complicated than that. She loved him, and she recognized that loving someone who was not prepared to love you in return could create all manner of hurt. That if she wasn't careful, she could become like her mother, and she didn't want that. Not in the least.

She wanted to avoid that at all costs.

Not because she didn't love her mother, but because she was able to recognize the mistakes her mother had made. She could recognize the things that had soured her, she hoped. Then try to avoid them.

But when she looked at him she worried. When she looked at him, she was concerned. Because what if he didn't… What if he couldn't. What if he would never love her in the way she loved him.

And what would that do to them. And what

would it do to her, and to their relationship with their children.

She knew about his deep wound. She knew about his darkest pain. But she wasn't sure even he fully understood the way that it had affected him.

She was just now getting to the bottom of how her own life had affected her, and all the things that she needed to put away. The things that her mother had been dealing with that she'd made about herself, because she was a child who hadn't known how to allow her mother to be human.

She could recognize that, and still also recognize that there were mistakes she didn't want to repeat with her own children. And the thing that she feared the most was becoming bitter over the lack of love. Except... She wondered if the key was being open. If it was being vulnerable. And that frightened her. How could it not. How could it not frighten her to ponder being open and vulnerable to a man who... Wasn't. He had moments of it. She felt that she had seen his truest self when he had thrust inside of her and growled and proclaimed that she was his.

She didn't want to be vulnerable alone. The thought was terrifying.

But also... She realized that she might have

to be. She realized that what she could not do was close down.

It would keep her from opening her heart to her children, wasn't that why it had taken her so long to feel joy in her pregnancy?

Joy.

Constantine was lying on the beach, the sun making his perfect skin gleam. She was hot, and she waded out into the water, and let the waves wash over her bare skin. She threw her arms out wide and looked up at the sky. And for the first time, she felt like there were no chains on her. No limits. She wasn't struggling. She had been given a gift, and she had felt some guilt over the fact that it was possible she might only be a better mother because of the access and wealth she'd been given.

But she realized then that wasn't it. She would be better because she would make the choice. Because she would choose joy even when it was hard. Because she would choose vulnerability, even when she wanted to protect herself.

Because she would choose love, even when it was easier to choose anger. And then, right then, she felt it. Shining in her soul like the sun, a beacon of light that she didn't think she could contain. She was going to be a mother. She was having twins.

She was married to the father of her children

and he was beautiful. An astonishing, wonderful man who had been through great pain. But who she knew had the capacity to care greatly too, because if he did not then his pain would not mark him so.

She gave herself permission. To feel all of her feelings. To luxuriate in them. She was having Constantine's babies. And she loved him. She loved him with everything that she was. And she would show him. Before she ever asked for anything else. She would show him. She would make herself vulnerable.

No matter the cost.

No matter the cost.

It was two days later that she asked to have an adventure.

"Am I not myself a great adventure, Morgan?" he asked.

She smiled. She loved him when he was arrogant. But now that she had given herself permission to use those words in her own heart, she found herself thinking she loved him all the time.

It was such an interesting thing, to be unfettered. And that was a gift from him. Not from his money, but from who he was innately.

This man who was so confident in and of

himself, and who looked at her like she was the stars.

That she had the power to test him and tempt him mattered to her.

But there was more to it than that even. He seemed to like everything about her, and to never be happier than when she was walking about naked.

He accepted admonishments from her, and allowed her to put sunblock on him, even though he insisted he was inured to the Greek sun, as a child of these lands.

He shared with her, even when he didn't want to. And there was something about that which made her feel grounded in her own importance. Which gave her the confidence to open herself up to feelings and desires she had previously kept closed off.

There was a wholeness to herself now.

She felt comfortable in her skin even as it expanded to accommodate the children she carried. Felt comfortable in her skin when he touched her, tasted her, did things to her that no other man ever had, and that she had never wanted another man to do.

It was more than being with someone who completed her. She was with someone who gave her the courage to complete herself. To be all that she was and accept it.

"Tell me about the parts of your industry," she said, while she watched him pack snacks for their adventure.

"Have we not discussed the company?"

"Not at length. Manufacturing and…"

"Real estate. Hotels."

"Really?"

"Yes."

"My degree is in hospitality. I'm very interested in that industry."

"I have several high-end resorts."

"I would like to visit them."

"Certainly."

"What if I… If I had ideas for them."

"Then you would be free to explore them."

"Really?"

"I enjoy talking to you, Morgan, and I enjoy your ideas. I imagine I would like them when applied to the resorts also."

"You wouldn't feel like I was invading your space."

A strange expression crossed his face. "No one in my family, other than my grandfather, has ever evinced the slightest bit of interest in the way we make money. It has always been me. The fact that you are interested in helping with that… It pleases me."

And she felt warmed by that. And by the idea

that she might find a way to use her degree, and her interests.

The island was such a beautiful jungle, and the hike they started out on was brilliant. Lush plants closing them in on the trail, making it all feel wild.

"You could be forgiven for thinking that a tiger might jump out at any moment," she said.

"The only predator here is me," he said, turning to flash a grin at her, and her stomach flipped. "I can guarantee you that."

"Funny how I'm not really afraid of you."

A shadow passed over his face, and he said nothing.

"It's a good thing we didn't hike naked," she said, dodging one of the plants. "It is a bit… Dense."

"Indeed. That is a recipe for certain disaster."

In fairness, nudity on sand could also be a bit of a disaster, but they had both risked it, and happily, to indulge themselves.

The trail wound deeper into the trees, until they were so thick the sun only peeked through in small patches, lending a prismatic effect to the jungle floor. The sound of the birds was held in by that canopy of trees, and they echoed loudly around them. There were bright blooms, pink and golden sapphire, a riot of color all around. And then she heard it. Rushing water.

"Where are we going?"

"You'll see."

When the trees cleared, her eyes widened.

It was a pool, clear as could be, with a massive, churning waterfall spilling into the depths of it from the top of the craggy rock.

The water was like crystal, and she could see little fish swimming down in the depths of it.

"This is…"

"This is the kind of opulence money does not buy," he said.

"In fairness, your money did buy the private island."

"But I have no control over this. I did not create it. Here my hand does not matter. There is no hand but God's."

"You don't like that, usually."

"I have been betrayed by it."

"But here you feel safe."

"It is not myself I fear for."

She put her hand on his face. "Of course not. I understand that."

They stood for a moment and looked at the water, and she knew, that this was the moment. She grabbed hold of the hem of her sundress and pulled it up over her head. She had no underwear on beneath.

She could feel his hot gaze on her as she

kicked off her shoes and slipped like a nymph into the pool.

"The water is wonderful," she said, swimming on her back until she was out at the center of it.

He was already removing his own clothing, and he dove in without making a splash, his movements neat and precise as always.

When he resurfaced, his dark eyes were intense. And she knew that she was looking at the predator. And she didn't mind. She swam away from him, kicking toward the waterfall. The water was a violent current at its base, and she avoided that, swimming behind it instead, where she found a massive, glimmering cavern.

"What is this?" she asked, and he came behind the falls with her.

"It's called Dead Man's Cove. Legend has it, there was a pirate treasure in here. But I believe the treasure is what's all around us."

"I believe it too." She got up out of the water, pleased to find the rock there smooth and sandy. He followed her, in all his naked glory. He was standing, and she on her knees. And she did not hesitate in her next action.

"I believe I found some treasure." She leaned in, sliding her tongue along the length of him, and his breath hissed through his teeth. He moaned as she took him into her mouth. As she began to pleasure him in the way that he had done for her so many times.

She had not been the boldest lover, but she was learning. He made her bold. In a way she had never been. She felt so changed, transformed. That she was the kind of woman who would take a man into her mouth outside. In a cave.

But it wasn't just because she wanted him. It wasn't that simple. It was because she loved him.

She pleasured him like that, her hands, her lips, her tongue. Until he was shaking. He grabbed hold of her hair, gritted his teeth. "Morgan. Wait."

But she didn't wait. She didn't stop. Until his control had shattered, fractured, until she had taken in every last drop of him. A forfeit of his control that she needed. For she was about to be more vulnerable than she had ever been. She looked up at him, her eyes meeting his, his expression one of supreme torture. And she smiled.

"I love you."

CHAPTER TWELVE

CONSTANTINE COULDN'T CATCH his breath. She had destroyed him. This wicked fairy who had taken him out to the middle of nowhere—*you took her out here*. Maybe he had. But he could scarcely remember now, and it hardly mattered. Because the world had turned upside down, and he no longer knew where he fit in it. Because Morgan was telling him that she loved him, and that was something he simply could not fathom. Something he could not abide by. She loved him.

How was such a thing possible?

She loved him.

His heart was thundering hard, and it wasn't just from his release.

He hadn't wanted it to end that way. He had wanted to pull away and thrust inside of her tight, welcoming body, but instead she had swallowed him down.

And it felt like she had won something. Like

she had stolen something he had fought his entire life for.

Control.

"I love you," she whispered.

"That is not necessary," he said.

"I don't care if it's necessary," she said. She looked up at him like he was… Pitiable. "Or rather, I don't care if you think it's necessary. It is. I've been thinking… I thought so much that I gave myself a headache. Trying to figure out how not to be the same sort of mother my own was. And then I talked to her. I did more thinking. And I found a lot of sympathy for her that I didn't have before. But it was when I stopped thinking and started feeling that I found the answers. She came across as bitter because she hardened herself. Because she let the things in her life that hurt her decide what she was allowed to feel. She let it put limits on her happiness. I don't want to do that. So this is me. Open and raw and vulnerable. This is me loving you. And I am better for it. I will be a better mother. And a better wife. And a better person."

"I can't," he said.

"I know you think you can't. But you don't have to know the answer. Not now. You don't need to tell me anything right now. And it wasn't… It wasn't an action item for you. It was a gift to myself."

"Morgan."

But she slipped away from the waterfall, back into the water, and she swam away, leaving him there, ragged and bloody and more uncertain than he had been since he was an eight-year-old boy, crying in the dungeon, uncertain if he would live to see tomorrow.

It took him time to figure out what he had to do. He sat up all night considering her words. She loved him. And the way that it had made him feel to hear it was disconcerting. It made his chest ache. And so did she. And he realized… He realized that he didn't need to be here with her. He needed to get his life in order. He had to deal with his parents head-on, and he had to go back to what he did best. Running the company. Here he had been on an endless vacation with her. Here, he had been ignoring who he was. He had allowed himself to get sucked into a fantasy. He had acknowledged as much days ago, but he hadn't realized how much this place had been affecting them until she had given him her declaration. She could feel what she wished. But he could not afford to change. He had promised her nothing would happen to her. And he meant that. He would protect her. With all that he was.

And that meant leaving her. But she would be here. She would be safe. He would send fully vetted staff and the doctor to care for her. And he would continue on as he should have this entire time. Because he knew where his strengths were. He handled things. He did not take care of people, not directly. He did not…

He took one last look at the house. And then he slung his bag over his shoulder and walked outside, down toward the yacht.

CHAPTER THIRTEEN

THINGS WERE NOT easy after that. Constantine was taking great pains to avoid her, after all of his proclamations about her being his. After... After everything.

He certainly wasn't acting as if she was his. Rather he was behaving like she was on the private island by herself.

And she had said that she didn't need anything from him, but she was very afraid that she actually did.

She wanted him to love her. Was that so bad?

And that was the problem. What she wanted was to be patient. What she wanted was to give him time.

But she also wanted the feeling of having her love returned, because she had felt so... Dry and lonely for all of her life, and even knowing her mother loved her it... It hadn't been expressed in a way that she could understand it, and so she had often felt like... Like it wasn't there. When she looked at Constantine, she could not imagine what he was thinking.

She was brooding in her room, upset that Constantine had been avoiding her for the better part of the day.

When she heard a door, she went to it. Expecting that it would be Constantine, because who else would it be? She was shocked to discover that it was not Constantine, but a woman.

"Hello, miss," she said. "I am Cristela. I am part of the household staff in Athens. I've been sent here to help care for you."

"What?"

"Mr. Kamaras has gone back home."

"He didn't."

"He did. He assures you that there is a phone waiting for you in what he was using as his office."

She ran straight upstairs to that office, and she looked in the phone to see if he had left his number. He had. She called him in absolute fury.

"Constantine," she said. "What is it you've done?"

"I'm leaving you on the island, where you are safe," he said. "But I... It was time for me to return back to work."

"You left me here."

"Yes."

"You're keeping me prisoner," she said.

"I am not. I'm making sure that you're safe. It is the only place on earth that I can make sure nothing will happen to you. And as the news of our relationship gets out…"

"This is… This is a lie. You were perfectly happy to be here with me until I told you that I loved you. And you left me. I think we both know it has more to do with that than it has to do with—"

"Are you calling me a coward?"

"Yes," she said. "I am. I'm calling you a coward because you deserve to be known as one. Because how dare you? How dare you leave me here?"

"You will be provided for. You will have everything that you could possibly want. And you have no reason to be upset."

"I have every reason to be upset," she said. "You have marooned me."

"On a private island with a beautiful house and a full staff. There is a doctor as well."

"Everything I could possibly want except the man that I love. You know that I… You had to know this would hurt me."

"The last thing I want to do is hurt you. I am protecting you."

"From yourself? Is this about your sister? Because I don't understand. You were a child, and you were kidnapped by very bad men. I can understand you being angry at your parents for not coming for you in time. Angry at your grandfather. I cannot understand you being angry at yourself for crying. You were a boy. A child."

"And the world does not care. The world does not care if you are innocent, if you are a child. It doesn't matter. There is great evil in the world, and it does not ask if you are prepared to grapple with it. It will be the same for our children. And I will protect you. Both of you, I will never fail again. Not as I have failed before."

"Do you really think that you failed? You didn't have control over those people. You didn't ask to have it happen to you. You never would have. They took you. They—"

"Enough. This is not a discussion. You are acting as if you've been abandoned, you have not been. I am taking care of you in the best way I ever could. That is my job. My task. It is not...distraction."

"Are you so afraid to be loved? Or are you just afraid of what it would be like if you love someone else again."

"I said it was enough. We do not need to have further discussion. You will remain on the island until after the birth of the children."

"And will you be here for the birth of the children?"

"I'm not a doctor. Such a thing is not necessary."

"And if it is for me?"

"You do not make the rules."

"And you don't care for me?"

"I did not say that."

"Then be honest with me. Be honest with yourself."

"We will speak again another time, Morgan. Perhaps I should've told you of my plans before I left. But I felt it would only result in unpleasantness."

"By unpleasantness you mean my feelings?"

"Feelings are unnecessary. What is necessary is protection."

He hung up the phone, and her heart felt scarred and bloodied. Bruised. She hadn't expected this. Of all the things, she hadn't expected this. She had been prepared. Prepared to love him with no certainty that he would love her back. Prepared to love him in spite of whether or not he loved her ever. But she had not been prepared to be abandoned. She had not been prepared to lose him.

She walked down the hall, and there was another member of staff, and then another. This place that had been theirs, the sanctuary, was now invaded with strangers, and she wanted to weep. It all felt wrong. Desperately, hideously wrong. She went into their room. His room, which had been theirs. And she lay down in the center of the bed and realized the linens had been changed and it didn't even smell like him anymore. And she gave in to her misery, clutching her belly and crying. How would she overcome this? How would she... How would this ever be okay?

It just would be. Because it had to be. Because she had to be. Because she would not let this wither her and make her bitter. She squeezed her eyes shut tight, and she tried to tell herself that, as she wept like she would never stop.

"And where is your wife?"

"Safe," Constantine said as he walked into the living room where his mother and father were already sitting. His mother would be upset. She would be devastated. But there was a reason he was doing this here. There was a reason he was doing it now.

"I'm here because I have to tell you something. Morgan's children are not Alex's. They are mine."

It was a truth that had to be told. He could not live in the lie. In the shelter of fantasy and neither should they.

They were his. And maybe the truth was... He needed his mother to know because he needed the children to matter. As his.

"Constantine," his father said, a warning tone that was almost funny on the old man who had never done an authoritative thing in his entire life.

"What are you saying?" his mother asked.

"I am saying that Morgan and I had an affair before Alex's death. The children are not his, they're mine."

"How can you be certain?"

"She was a virgin when she came to me."

"That makes no sense," his mother said.

"It may not make sense, but it is the truth."

"How dare you," his mother said. "How dare you take this from me."

And he knew it was time. To hear all of the things that he was certain his parents thought.

"You took Athena from us. You did. You took her. And now Alex's gone and…"

"And you wish it was me who were dead," he said. "I know. I have always known."

His mother's eyes went wide with horror. "I did not say that."

"But it is what you feel."

"No," she said. "I wish none of my children were dead. I wish none of my children were dead and I… I wish I could go back in time and change whatever I need to change in order to make it so that you… So that you are all okay."

"That isn't what you were going to say."

"No. It isn't. Because what I was going to say was hideously unfair and I didn't even mean it. Because I want to be angry at someone, and if you were the one in the grave then it would be Alex that I was yelling at, because I would be yelling at whoever remained. Because it is all bad. It is bad and horrible and nothing but grief, and there is nothing that fixes it."

"Except having Alex's children would have fixed it."

"No," she said. "They still wouldn't be Alex. And you… You're going to be a father."

"Yes," he said, gritting his teeth, not certain what the hell he was supposed to make of this new development. Because he had been waiting for the recriminations that had nearly come, but then they had stopped. Because he had been waiting to be told that he was a disgrace, and she had nearly said it. Because it would excuse him. If they blamed him, then it would excuse him from ever having to deal with any of this. Because blame was so much easier than the reality of what he had. Which was loss and fear and guilt. Which were all things he could not control. Blame was focused. Guilt was such an easy thing to keep. It was the other emotions he didn't want. The other emotions he didn't want to have a handle on.

"They are your children," she said. "And you

will love them. Even if you don't want to. Even if it feels dangerous. And I will love them too."

"Mother…"

"It's true, Constantine. You will."

"I don't want this. I don't want any of it. I didn't set out to get his girlfriend pregnant. I never would have… I…"

"Where is she?"

"She's on the island. I have to keep her safe."

"So you've imprisoned her."

She was using that same word to describe what he'd done that Morgan had already used.

"I'm keeping her safe. I am doing what I was asked to do, and none of you understand that. You do not…take care of the family business. Just as you did not watch us when we were on the beach." His mother drew back as if he'd struck her. "Grandfather told me it was my job to be the man. To keep the family together and I have done so. I cannot afford to be distracted."

His mother looked away, then back at him. "Are you keeping her safe? The family? Or are you keeping yourself safe?"

"Enough. I needed to tell you the truth of the matter. She is my wife and she is my wife in truth. The children are mine. But that is all I came for."

"Your grandfather was a hard man," his father said. "I know. He raised me. He was broken by the loss of Athena, and he loved you very much, but he…he was worried. He was worried your experience would make you soft, traumatized, and I was furious at him when I heard him give you that command to be a man when you were only a boy."

"You were still acting as a boy," Constantine said, hard. "What was I to do?"

His father's shoulders slumped. "I have never been the man my father would have wanted. I admire you and your work ethic, Constantine. But surely…surely there must be balance? Perhaps I could have done more. But must you do everything?"

Yes.

"It is not a debate. It is simply what is," Constantine said.

"Will you go back to her now?" his father asked.

"I will go back to work."

He got into his car and he began to drive. And panic overtook him. A strange, clawing panic he had not felt since he was a child.

And this, he realized was what was underneath the guilt all along. This, he realized was the real thing that drove him.

Fear.

Because you could be a child who had been getting ice cream one moment but was snatched off the streets the next. A child who watched early-morning cartoons with your sister, and then one day she was gone and you never saw her again. And they said it was your fault. *Your fault.*

A curve came up quicker than he expected and he swerved, his car spinning out and nearly going into a ditch. And he sat there in the middle of the road, clutching the steering wheel, his heart beating hard.

And he realized. He realized.

He would live with this fear for the rest of his life. And keeping her on an island wouldn't solve it.

And she was... She was brave enough to love him. She was brave enough, and she was... Brave enough to raise the children in a way that he never could.

The answer was not to keep her locked away tightly.

The answer was to let her go.

CHAPTER FOURTEEN

SHE HAD BEEN alone on the island for three weeks. Every day that she felt the babies move, that she ate breakfast alone and lunch and then dinner. That she swam by herself and felt nearly blinded by the constant beauty, she missed him. She was in a rage.

Every day.

She was furious that he had done this to her. But he had done it to them.

How dare he? Really, how very dare he.

But he wasn't here for her to yell at. And that just added to the indignation of it all.

And then, when she was taking her breakfast one morning, she saw a yacht in the distance and was certain that she was hallucinating. Absolutely certain.

But no, it kept coming, closer and closer. Until there he was. And it took all of her strength not to run out into the sea to greet him. But he wasn't smiling when he moored the boat. Rather his expression was grim. "I'm sorry," he said by way of greeting.

"You're sorry?"

"Yes. And I've come to… To apologize and set you free."

"Set me free?"

"I cannot keep you here on the island. I also cannot keep you with me."

"Why not?" She felt plaintive and silly and sad. Angry at herself for being hopeful, even for a moment.

"Because I cannot. Because to stay with you is to live with fear. And I cannot do it. Not anymore."

"Being with me makes you fearful?"

"Yes," he said. "Because if there's one thing I know, I cannot protect anyone from the cruelty of this world. And I thought to keep you prisoner. I thought to keep you safe that way. But then I realized… I am the one who cannot handle it. Not you. I will never… I will never take the children to learn to swim, or to the beach. Or to get ice cream. Because I will only ever be able to think of the terror that awaits them. And that is all. That is all their life will ever be. Living with a man who knows only how to keep people in chains to keep them safe."

"So you would keep yourself in chains instead?"

His eyes were wild, and she felt a great stab of horrible sympathy when he looked at her. "I'm not in chains." He shook his head. "I am a man in full control when you were not in my life. I never had an issue with this as long as you weren't there."

"You love me," she said.

"No," he said.

"You do. It's why you're afraid for me. The same reason you're afraid for the children. You love me, and you grieve the fact that you have feelings. But you do. And there's nothing that can be done about them. Except to give in to them."

"No."

"Why do you only trust fate when it's bad? Why are you so convinced there is evil under every rock, when there is love right here?"

"Because I cannot guarantee—"

"I never asked for your guarantees. I don't want them. I want you. We must live dangerous. We must live dangerous in order to live free. Or you become hard like my mother, you end up having everything, and being able to enjoy none of it. My mother had me, and I was desperate for her love, and she couldn't show it because of her fear. Because of the way that my father had hurt her. And you... You are letting the men that took you, the men that took your sister from you decide how happy you will be. Why would you give them that power?"

His throat worked, stark emotion filling his dark eyes.

"You are allowed to have feelings. It is not weak. You wept because you missed your sister. You wept out of fear for her. You were not wrong for doing that. You were not wrong for loving her any more than you are wrong for loving me."

"But this cannot be…"

"I'm afraid it is," she said. "I'm afraid you love me. And you can send me away, but you will still love me. And you can keep your children at a distance, and you will love them. It will just be locked in a cage inside of you. And what kind of a tribute is that? To your sister. To your brother. And to your own self. You're alive, Constantine. We are alive. Why can we not love?"

"I was tasked with being…with being the one to keep us all together. My grandfather told me…"

"And why do you care about doing what he said? Because you love him. But he was still wrong. My mother was wrong and she loved me. Love doesn't make people perfect. It doesn't make the world perfect. But we don't have to wait for perfection to find happiness."

And then Constantine fell to his knees and wrapped his arms around her. "I love you," he said, the words broken. "I love you."

"I know," she said, smoothing his dark hair off his face. "I really do."

"But it opens you up to so much pain," he said.

"The pain is there, whether we protect ourselves from it or not. The only thing we ever managed to really keep out is the joy."

"No more," he said.

She nodded her head. "No more."

"I love you Morgan," he said.

"I love you too."

"Let us go to bed."

"Yes. I think that's a good idea."

The phone woke Constantine in the middle of the night. But he was too sated by his evening spent with Morgan to be angry. He answered, and it was his mother on the other end, her voice breathless and strained.

"What is it?"

"It's Athena," she said. "They've found Athena."

And the last bit of any defense he had built

up inside of him crumbled completely. And the emotion he had been holding back for all those years poured out.

Athena was rescued by a man called Castor Xenakis who had been searching for his own sister for years. It was an incredible story of persistence, and he had apparently found his own love with a woman named Glory along the way. But when his work had come to fruition they had discovered that more than one girl had been kept by the wife of this particular crime lord, a woman who had always wanted daughters.

Apparently there had been a tip from a man known only as Dante, which seemed a bit on the nose, if it was a reference to *The Inferno*. But the end result was simply that he'd helped save Athena, whether he was a devil or not.

Athena looked far younger than Constantine did, her glossy dark hair smooth and perfect, her skin golden like the rest of her family, but with a pale cast, as if she did not spend very much time in the sun.

"These are strange times," she said.

"Do you remember me?" Constantine asked, his voice rough.

And Morgan's heart felt bruised on behalf of her husband.

"Of course, Constantine." And though it was

tentative, Athena smiled. "Do you remember, we used to watch that cartoon about ponies."

And Morgan wept. Her heart had never felt so full of joy.

And she was grateful. For the decision to open her heart in the first place. For her decision to love even when it was hard.

And she no longer worried about being a good mother. She knew she would be. She didn't worry, because she was happy with herself. Happy with the wife she was. And she had a sister-in-law. One that she was very excited to get to know.

She and Constantine went to bed that night in his room. The room where they had first made love.

"It is a miracle," he said.

"You see," she said. "Sometimes the miraculous is hiding just around the corner. Not everything is dark."

"And sometimes the miraculous is right in plain sight," he said, looking directly at her. "As you were, from the beginning. From the first moment I saw you."

"I love you."

"I love you too."

"Do you think this will help, with the fear?"

"You know, you already had."

"Me?"

"Yes. Love and fear cannot occupy the same space. And by choosing one I had already let go of the other. That was because of you. Athena is just an extra gift."

"And what an amazing gift."

"Yes. Indeed." He kissed her mouth. "It seems the gift of love is one that keeps on giving."

EPILOGUE

MORGAN WONDERED IF someone could burst from happiness. If they could, she would. When she gave birth to the twins, she was exhausted, but euphoric.

"And do you have names picked out for them?"

He nodded. "If you don't mind, I would like to name them Alexius and Athena."

Athena, the proud aunt, was in the room, beaming.

"I would like that," she said.

"We don't have to. If you fear the names might be cursed."

"I don't fear that. There's far too much love for a curse to continue to exist."

"On that, my dear wife, we can agree."

"Perhaps it is fate that we should be happy," she said.

"I heard it said once, we do not have to wait for perfection to claim happiness."

"I said that."

He smiled. "But I believe we may have found perfection."

She kissed him, all the love in her heart pouring out of her like a wave. She was vulnerable, and so was he. And she was overjoyed. "I believe, my dearest husband, you are right."

* * * * *

Enchanted by
His Secretly Pregnant Cinderella?
Get lost in these other Millie Adams stories!

The Scandal Behind the Italian's Wedding
Stealing the Promised Princess
Crowning His Innocent Assistant
The Only King to Claim Her

Available now!